FAST TRACK

Books By Lee Goldberg

Calico
Crown Vic
King City
The Walk
Watch Me Die
McGrave
Three Ways to Die

The Sharpe & Walker Series

Malibu Burning
Ashes Never Lie
Hidden in Smoke

The Eve Ronin Series

Lost Hills
Bone Canyon
Gated Prey
Movieland
Dream Town
Fallen Star

The Ian Ludlow Thrillers

True Fiction
Killer Thriller
Fake Truth

The Fox & O'Hare Series (coauthored with Janet Evanovich)

Pros & Cons (novella)
The Shell Game (novella)
The Heist
The Chase
The Job
The Scam
The Pursuit

The Diagnosis Murder Series

The Silent Partner
The Death Merchant
The Shooting Script
The Waking Nightmare
The Past Tense
The Dead Letter
The Double Life
The Last Word

The Monk Series

Mr. Monk Goes to the Firehouse
Mr. Monk Goes to Hawaii
Mr. Monk and the Blue Flu
Mr. Monk and the Two Assistants
Mr. Monk in Outer Space
Mr. Monk Goes to Germany
Mr. Monk Is Miserable
Mr. Monk and the Dirty Cop
Mr. Monk in Trouble

Mr. Monk Is Cleaned Out
Mr. Monk on the Road
Mr. Monk on the Couch
Mr. Monk on Patrol
Mr. Monk Is a Mess
Mr. Monk Gets Even

The Charlie Willis Series

My Gun Has Bullets
Dead Space

The Dead Man Series (coauthored with William Rabkin)

Face of Evil
Ring of Knives (with James Daniels)
Hell in Heaven
The Dead Woman (with David McAfee)
The Blood Mesa (with James Reasoner)
Kill Them All (with Harry Shannon)
The Beast Within (with James Daniels)
Fire & Ice (with Jude Hardin)
Carnival of Death (with Bill Crider)
Freaks Must Die (with Joel Goldman)
Slaves to Evil (with Lisa Klink)
The Midnight Special (with Phoef Sutton)
The Death March (with Christa Faust)
The Black Death (with Aric Davis)
The Killing Floor (with David Tully)
Colder Than Hell (with Anthony Neil Smith)
Evil to Burn (with Lisa Klink)
Streets of Blood (with Barry Napier)

Crucible of Fire (with Mel Odom)
The Dark Need (with Stant Litore)
The Rising Dead (with Stella Green)
Reborn (with Kate Danley, Phoef Sutton, and Lisa Klink)

The Jury Series

Judgment
Adjourned
Payback
Guilty

Nonfiction

The Best TV Shows You Never Saw
Unsold Television Pilots 1955–1989
Television Fast Forward
Science Fiction Filmmaking in the 1980s (cowritten with
William Rabkin, Randy Lofficier, and Jean-Marc Lofficier)
*The Dreamweavers: Interviews with Fantasy Filmmakers
of the 1980s* (cowritten with William Rabkin,
Randy Lofficier, and Jean-Marc Lofficier)
Successful Television Writing (cowritten with William Rabkin)
The Joy of Sets: Interviews on the Sets of 1980s Genre Movies
*The James Bond Films 1962–1989: Interviews
with the Actors, Writers and Directors*

FAST TRACK

LEE GOLDBERG

CUTTING EDGE

ISBN-13: 978-1-962896-62-7
Cover design by Jeroen Ten Berge

Published by
Cutting Edge Books
PO Box 8212
Calabasas, CA 91372

To Valerie and Madison

PROLOGUE

Line up five golden retrievers and it wouldn't take you long to see that although they might look exactly the same, they've each got their own unique personalities. And from their barks or whines or the way they ran around, you'd know if they were happy or sad or if they wanted to lick your face or if they wanted to tear it off.

Katie Reed believed cars were a lot like dogs. If you parked five identical Corvettes in front of her and started their engines, in a few minutes she'd know how they drove and what their quirks were just by listening. She'd also know if they'd drive smoothly or break apart into fiery death traps.

And if she looked closer, studied the dings in the paint, the creases in the upholstery, the stains on the carpet, the wear on the steering wheel, and the smoothing of the tire treads, she'd know not only the history of the cars, but all about the lives of the people who owned them.

That was her gift, though it'd be hard to argue whether it was nature or nurture that was responsible for it, since she'd spent most of her nineteen years on this earth in her daddy's garage.

If Katie *really* wanted to know a car, to transform a charmless Japanese compact into an ass-kicking, asphalt-melting, crowd-pleasing street-racing machine, she'd work on it late at night, when all the other mechanics were gone and she had the garage to herself, which was often, since she and her older brother, Stephen, lived in the apartment upstairs.

It wasn't the nicest place to live, smack in an industrial corner of Reseda, south of Ventura Boulevard in the San Fernando Valley, but it was the cheapest, across the street from a U-Store-It and bordered by a plumbing supply company, a lumber yard, and the back of a 7-Eleven.

It was after 1 a.m., and Katie was in her grease-stained mechanics' overalls, leaning under the hood of a Subaru Impreza that was manufactured for fuel economy and that she was transforming with mad scientist zeal into a gas-guzzling speed demon. The other four bays in the cinder-block garage were filled with three street racers in various states of repair or transformation and one car hidden under a filthy tarp.

Katie was bikini-model thin, though she ate like a truck driver, and had strong arms and shoulders from a lifetime of working with engines, though her baggy overalls didn't reveal much of her shape. She had long brown hair that she tied in a ponytail and bunched up under a dirty baseball cap.

But her sultry beauty came through no matter how hard she tried to hide it, and she *did* try, because she saw it as a detriment to being taken seriously in the male-dominated world of high-performance cars. Some men figured that because she masked her femininity and worked with cars, she was a lesbian. She wasn't, but she didn't mind them making the mistake, since those who did were usually boneheaded Neanderthals or assholes anyway.

She was wrestling with a bolt that didn't want to move, putting all her strength into it, when it suddenly gave, and she lost her grip on the wrench, slicing the palm of her right hand on a sharp edge in the bowels of the engine.

Katie swore and yanked her hand out, glaring at the car as if it had harmed her intentionally. She looked like a petulant, freckle-faced child who'd been nipped by the family dog, and for just a moment, her face lost the hard-edged maturity and determination that gave her the authority, beyond her co-ownership of the garage with Stephen, to boss around mechanics more than twice her age.

She examined her hand. There was a nasty gash across the palm. She grabbed a clean rag and tied it across her hand. It would do for now. She was cinching up the knot when the sound of a car approaching caught her attention. She cocked her head and stood very still, her eyes staring out into the darkness.

Katie heard a car door slam, then the hoarse, guttural wheeze as the unseen car sped off. She turned just as her brother, Stephen, two years her senior, came straggling in, his broad shoulders slumped in anger and defeat. With his blond hair, deep tan, and lean body, he looked as if he'd grown up on the beach, riding the waves, and not in the flats of the valley, riding asphalt.

"What happened to our car, Stephen?"

"What makes you think something happened to it?"

He made a beeline towards the row of lockers, opening up his own. Katie followed him.

"Because somebody with a lot of attitude and not enough money to support it just dropped you off in a VW Corrado G6o."

Stephen pulled off his sweat-stained T-shirt, threw it in the locker, and pulled out a fresh one. "It was a Honda CRX."

"The hell it was. I'd have to be deaf not to recognize a small-displacement four-banger with a stock G-Lader supercharger, which is about to crap out because your idiot friends installed a smaller pulley in a lame effort to get more boost."

Steve put on his shirt and glared at her. "You expect me to believe that you got all of that from the sound of the engine?"

"It's not a bad car, if all you want to do is give your grand-mother a ride to the hairdresser. But they ought to stop using synthetic oil."

"You can't hear that."

"I can smell it. The engine is so tired the synthetic is weeping past the seals and burning on the exhaust."

"Now you're just making this shit up."

She crossed her arms under her chest. "Where's our RX-7?"

"Gone."

"You crashed it?"

"I lost it."

She stared at him in smoldering fury. "You raced for keys?"

Stephen shrugged. "I didn't have any cash."

She shoved him hard, slamming him back into the lockers. "So you thought betting our car was the solution? The RX was all we had left."

"Relax, it's no big deal."

"We're broke, Stephen. Every penny Dad left us is gone."

"Because it was only pennies."

"You're not listening to me. We could lose the garage. It meant everything to him."

"A lot more than we did." Stephen started to move past her.

Katie cut him off and got right in his face. "It means everything *to me.* How could you do this?"

Her words stung, and it showed on his face as if he'd been slapped. "I'd rather live on the edge than wait to get pushed off of it."

"In other words, you're a selfish asshole."

"I can win the car back, Katie. I can do it tonight before the engine is even cold."

"With *what*? You don't even have a car to drive."

Stephen looked past her to the car under the tarp. She followed his gaze.

"No," she said.

He headed for the wall outside the front office, where dozens of car keys dangled from numbered hooks on a pegboard. Katie chased after him, but he got there first, snatching a set of keys before she could reach them herself, then held his hand away from her.

"It's Dad's car," she said.

"I'm sick of seeing it here. It's like his tombstone."

"Don't make it yours."

He shouldered his way past her and whipped the tarp off the car, revealing a lovingly restored red '71 DeTomaso Pantera, the wedge-nosed, midengine, supersleek offspring of a doomed romance between a brokenhearted Ford Motor Company, on the rebound from harsh rejection by Ferrari, and a car-making company created by Formula One race car driver Alejandro DeTomaso and designer Tom Tjaarda. The result was a poor man's Lamborghini, with the cool lines of an Italian sports car and the deadly unreliability of a Ford Pinto. It was so poorly designed that drivers had to take their shoes off to use the pedals. Elvis Presley got so pissed off with his Pantera that he shot it to death with a handgun.

But the car was sex on wheels to look at and could go from zero to sixty in four seconds and top 180 miles per hour, so who really cared if it was about as safe to drive as a truck full of perspiring sticks of dynamite? The danger only added to the thrill of driving the car. It was like dating a bisexual supermodel with an insatiable appetite for sex, partying, and heroin. The flameout was inevitable, but oh, what fun she'd be until then.

Stephen got into the car and started the engine. The car roared to life, causing the needle on the green-on-black tachometer to tremble. There were more gauges on the dash than in the cockpit of a fighter jet. He looked up at Katie, his hand on the wheel.

"Dad always said it's not about controlling the car. It's about controlling yourself."

"That's why he never raced it. That's why you shouldn't."

"I'm not Dad," he said.

"Yeah," she said. "You're still alive."

He shook his head, dismissing her comment, and sped off, peeling rubber as he made the turn out of the garage, sped through the parking lot, and jackknifed onto the street, leaving a trail of sparks and rubber.

She was still listening to the fading sound of the engine when she noticed that her hand was bleeding, the blood dripping onto the floor and seeping into the cracks in the concrete.

Stephen should have listened to his sister. Two hours later, in a street race in downtown Los Angeles, he lost control of the Pantera in a tight turn and spun out into a utility pole that cleaved the car in half and decapitated him.

Nobody called 911. Instead, all the drivers and spectators fled, emptying the streets along the racing route within five minutes. The smoking wreckage wasn't discovered until dawn, when a bus driver reported the accident.

Stephen's remains were delivered to Witten & Sons mortuary in Canoga Park. The remains of the car were towed to Katie's garage.

CHAPTER ONE

If you were to compare a photograph of the garage taken three years ago, the night Stephen Reed drove off to his gruesome death, with one from today, the differences would be subtle, perhaps details only a car lover would notice.

Before, all the cars in the garage were urban street racers, in the midst of being either built or maintained or repaired. There still are street racers in the shop, but now they share space with a car under a filthy tarp, an out-of-warranty Ford Explorer, and a Toyota Camry, rides for a commuting dad and a soccer mom, getting new brakes or hoses, because it's good for cash flow.

Katie looks much the same, still unable to camouflage her beauty in engine grease and baggy mechanics' overalls, but she's got an edge now, a touch of cynicism and stoniness in her that wasn't there before. You can see it in her brown eyes and the rigid way she's sitting on the edge of her office desk, only inches away from Warren Kester, a man her age but who appears older because he's wearing an off-the-rack jacket and tie from Men's Wearhouse that look like something a funeral home might buy to dress an elderly corpse.

To Katie, there's something adorable about Warren. He looks like a child dressing up as an adult, maybe because she's known him since high school.

Warren is holding a briefcase upright on his lap like a shield.

And for good reason.

"I've done everything that I can—but the bank is adamant this time," Warren says. "If we don't get the fifty-thousand-dollar payment in seven days, we'll foreclose on the garage."

"You'd really do that to me?"

Warren scrunches a little bit behind the pitiful protection of his briefcase, which, by the way, holds his iPhone, a granola bar, and a *People* magazine. "It's not me. It's the bank."

"You *are* the bank, Warren."

"To you I am. But the truth is, I'm just a lowly account executive. If I give you another extension, they'll fire me."

"You could get another job," Katie says, glancing at the wall behind Warren, which is covered with family photos, some yellowing and curling with age. "But this garage is irreplaceable."

Warren sits up now, feeling a flash of anger. "Do you really expect me to sacrifice my career for you?"

She puts her hands on her knees and leans towards him with a smile. "You would if you loved me."

Warren flushes with embarrassment because he's had a crush on her since kindergarten, and now his face has betrayed him, which embarrasses him even more. He gets up, still holding the briefcase in front of him. He'd like to hide his flushed face behind it.

"I've done everything I can do," he says, backing towards the office door that leads into the garage. "I'm sorry, Katie. It isn't anything personal."

"Everything about this garage is personal to me."

"Maybe that's the problem." It's true, but Warren still regrets it the moment he says it. So he avoids her gaze and leaves.

She sighs and glances at the pictures on the wall again. In one of them, her father stands grinning beside the Pantera he'd just begun to restore. The captured moment crackles with enthusiasm, happiness, and the promise of dreams yet to come true.

That promise was broken.

"How did it go with the bank?" The words seem to come from a throat filled with gravel.

Katie turns to see a mechanic standing in the doorway. It's Schmitty, a German-born ex-hippie who looks like Willie Nelson in mechanics' overalls, his face and voice weathered by seventy years of hard living, hard loving, and hard drinking. His skin is like tan leather upholstery worn down over time from heavy use. There's gray stubble on his craggy face, and his long, gray-flecked hair is held back from his face by a bandana tied in a knot on the back of his head.

She forces a smile. "It went great, Schmitty. They were impressed by my business plan and seduced by my charm. I managed to reconsolidate the debt and work out a new payment schedule with them."

"I thought that's what you did last month."

"And I did it again this month. That's how good I am."

Schmitty smiles. He knows the truth and how much it hurts her. But he also knows how to raise her spirits, if only for a few minutes.

"The crew is getting hungry, so I was thinking we should have a couple of pizzas delivered."

She breaks into a broad, mischievous smile. "That a great idea, Schmitty."

There have never been two people more excited about ordering a pizza.

In Tarzana, a few miles west of Katie's garage, a silver Audi A6 with dark tinted windows is idling at the curb outside a storefront insurance agency in a strip mall on Ventura. At the wheel of the car is Wolf, an odd name for a muscled, bald young man who keeps himself hairless, regularly shaving and waxing himself in his free time. He looks like an uncircumcised penis with a face drawn on it and that's fine by him. Right now, he is listening to music on his iPod and glancing impatiently at the storefront, wedged between a donut shop and a dry cleaner.

They don't actually sell insurance at that insurance agency. What they do is take bets. It's a front for a mob bookmaking operation.

And in the back room right now, three hooded thugs toting automatic weapons are robbing the place, stuffing piles of cash into gym bags. They are Marcu, Axel, and Clem, guys who like the thrill of the robbery even more than the money they are being paid to pull it off.

In that regard, they are a lot like Shank, one of the six guys lying facedown on the floor. Under his hoodie and baggy jeans, Shank is tattooed from neck to toe with skulls, snakes, and naked women with huge tits. He's not the kind of guy who is going to forgive or forget this.

A few blocks north of Katie's garage is Ventura Boulevard, the Champs Élysées of Encino. Both are wide, long boulevards lined with Burger Kings, Pizza Huts, movie theaters, and car dealerships. What this stretch of Ventura Boulevard doesn't usually have that the Champs Élysées *does* is class and French women, but today there's Nicole Devereaux, Paris-born and raised and some lucky man's very hot, very young trophy wife, the natural blond driver of the red Ferrari California that's parked on a sidewalk just west of Reseda Boulevard.

And standing there beside her car, in her skintight cap-sleeve Herve Leger bandage dress, showing off the only authentic cleavage in the 818 area code, Nicole is a jaw-dropping distraction to every man stuck in the traffic on Ventura Boulevard, except for the man she's facing.

That man happens to be freshly minted LAPD Detective Eric Visnjic. He's pointedly ignoring Nicole's obvious charms. He's the twentysomething guy who, with his overweight fiftysomething partner, Harry Prendergast, just pulled Nicole over.

Strictly speaking, it's not their job to cite people for traffic violations, but Nicole's was too flagrant even for the detectives to overlook, especially Eric, who has only recently graduated from wearing a uniform, riding a patrol car, and writing tickets all day. Some habits die hard. Besides, now Harry gets to sit in their unmarked Crown Vic and ogle Nicole all he wants while he finishes his Subway sandwich and large Coke. It's like watching Cinemax soft-core porn in his La-Z-Boy recliner, something he does almost every night.

Eric looks at her license, as if there might be something on the card that will explain why this woman thought it was a good idea to drive her Ferrari down the sidewalk instead of the street.

"Here in the United States, Ms. Devereaux, the sidewalks are where the people go," Eric says, as he begins writing up her ticket. "The streets are where the cars go."

"But the cars aren't going, so I had to use the sidewalk." She says it in a matter-of-fact way, as if what she did was common sense instead of pure insanity, which only makes Eric more frustrated as he writes. He believes in playing by the rules.

"You could have killed someone."

"Only if it was someone too stupid to move out of the way, so I would have been doing our species a favor by taking the idiot out of the gene pool. Think of it as natural selection."

"Think of it as a big fine."

He tears out the ticket and hands it to her with her license. She glances at the ticket.

"You call that a big fine?"

"Would you like me to ticket you for some more violations?"

She shrugs. "If that's what gets you off, and judging by the way you've pressed and starched that shirt, I'd say that it does."

Eric hears a laugh and glances back at the car at Harry, who likes it when people give his uptight partner a hard time. He turns back to Nicole.

"Don't push it, lady."

"Pushing it is what makes life fun, Officer. You ought to try it some time."

Eric goes back to his car and gets into the driver's seat. He and Harry watch Nicole as she slips into her Ferrari like it's something she's wearing.

"She thinks she owns the world," Eric says.

"She does."

"Just because she's young, rich, and has a killer body?"

"What else is there?" Harry says.

Eric puts the car into reverse and backs up to the entrance to a parking lot, turns the car so it faces the street, and drives off.

Nicole watches them go in her rearview mirror with an amused smile on her face, then starts her car. Or tries to. It won't start. Her smile turns into a frown. Yet another annoying inconvenience. This day is going to hell. She sighs, takes out her iPhone, and makes a call to AAA's Roadside Assistance.

"I need a tow truck," she tells the operator, and then, as an afterthought, "And an espresso. Make it snappy."

Roughly midway between the spot where hot Nicole's Ferrari is stalled and penis-head Wolf is waiting for his friends to finish their robbery, you'll find Sal's Pizza, a carryout place with a fading banner in the window that promises "Pizza from Our Door to Yours in 30 Minutes … or It's FREE!"

Those pizzas are delivered this afternoon by Mike Cassidy, who is arriving right now on one of Sal's fleet of three aging

Vespa scooters with a stack of pizza warmers attached to the rear rack with bungee cords.

He's wearing a Sal's Pizza denim jacket, with a smiling pizza-face logo and a phone number emblazoned on the back, and an enormous yellow helmet painted to look like the top of a cheese pizza. Mike might as well be wearing a clown costume and he knows it. But he needs the job and at least isn't trapped in a building all day.

He's six feet tall and naturally easygoing and has the kind of rugged good looks that cry out for a cowboy hat and boots to go with his T-shirt and jeans. It's because of those looks that he can wear Sal's ridiculous outfit and ride that tiny scooter and not be humiliated. To everyone who sees him, it comes off like he's in on a joke instead of being one. Not many people could manage that, and certainly not without lots of effort, but Mike does it without trying at all. Maybe because he's comfortable enough with who he is that he doesn't care about how others see him. And maybe that's why he may be perpetually broke, but he has no trouble getting laid by the sexiest woman in any room he happens to be in.

He strides into the pizza place and passes the empty warmers over the counter to Sal, a guy in his sixties who looks like he eats one pizza for every ten that he makes and, because of that and his rosy-red cheeks, is drafted every Christmas by some local community group to be Santa Claus. Sal is not happy as he slides two pizzas into the warmers.

"You were three minutes late delivering that last pie."

"What kind of prick calls to complain about a pizza that's three minutes late?" Mike asks.

"The kind who wants something for free, which is everybody on earth. That's two pies you've cost me this month."

"They didn't cost you anything, Sal. You took them out of my paycheck."

"If you keep making late deliveries, you won't have a paycheck." Sal hands over the pizza warmers and a slip of paper to Mike. "You've got fifteen minutes left to deliver these. You think you can make it?"

Mike glances at the paper. The address is for Reed's Garage. He smiles to himself. "I can do it hopping on one foot."

He hurries to his Vespa, packs the pizzas, and heads off.

The three thugs run out of the insurance agency, lugging their AK-47s and gym bags stuffed with money, and collide right with a woman on her way out of the bakery, sending her and her two dozen donuts flying onto the street. She sees their guns and starts screaming.

The guys throw their stuff into the car and jump inside, and Wolf peels away without waiting for them to even close their doors. That tire-smoking takeoff only adds to the excitement the three guys are feeling. They are on a post-robbery high, jacked up on adrenaline and juicing for more.

"You should have seen those pussies on the floor," Marcus says, sitting beside Wolf. "They were crapping themselves."

But Wolf isn't listening. He's still wearing his earbuds as he casually weaves at high speed eastbound on Ventura, swerving into oncoming traffic to get around the slow cars.

One of those cars happens to be an unmarked LAPD sedan.

"What the hell?" Eric hits the siren, makes a screeching U-turn, and tears off after the Audi, not waiting for an okay from Harry, who catches his Coke before it falls out of the cup holder and spills all over his crotch.

"When did we become traffic cops?" Harry says and puts on his seat belt. But before he can complain any more, the call comes from the dispatcher, alerting all units in the area to three armed individuals fleeing the scene of an apparent robbery in a silver Audi. "Fuck. Try not to go too fast."

Eric floors the gas pedal, pinning Harry into his seat with a sudden burst of speed.

Axel and Clem, the two thugs in the backseat of the Audi, turn and look as the unmarked cop car, lights flashing behind the front grill and siren wailing, closes in on them.

"Oh shit, Wolf, it's the cops," Axel says. "Do something."

"I'm doing it," Wolf says. He is totally calm. Fact is, he's enjoying this. He yanks the wheel and heads north on Corbin.

While this chase is going on, a few blocks away Mike Cassidy is heading to Katie's garage, or at least he's trying to. His path north on Tampa is blocked by a slow-moving lime-green Toyota Camry that won't get out of his way. Whatever direction Mike goes, the Camry veers into his path.

So Mike, frustrated, makes an abrupt right turn down an alley, cutting across towards Reseda Boulevard.

Eric is driving confidently and intently. Harry is buckled in tight, hands on the dash, as if he's riding a roller coaster. They are closing in on the Audi. Soon Eric can try to initiate a pit maneuver, tapping the Audi's rear bumper with his, and spin the son of a bitch into a streetlight. That would be fun.

"Slow down," Harry says.

"I don't want to lose him."

"It's better than crashing."

"We won't," Eric says.

That's when a black-and-white blasts out of a side street, slipping between the two cars.

"Shit!" Eric yells, swerving to avoid rear-ending the cop in front of him.

"We can leave it to the uniforms now," Harry says.

"They're going to need backup."

The Audi makes a hard right, taking a side street east towards Tampa.

Mike checks his watch. It's 1:25. He's got only five minutes left. He looks up just as a tow truck carrying a red Ferrari cuts him off, blocking his way to Reseda Boulevard. He makes a U-turn, doubles back to another northbound street, and speeds off.

If he'd happened to glance at the tow truck cab, he would have seen Nicole Devereaux in the passenger seat, happily sipping her espresso.

There's roadwork being done on the street ahead of Wolf: an open ditch, utility trucks, and workers all around. No way he can go through. So he's got to make a sudden, very tight, high-speed turn at the intersection that's right before the construction.

No problem.

Wolf shifts gears, punches the gas, pulls the hand brake, and pops the clutch, expertly steering his car into a drift, sliding around the curve as if skating on ice, hugging the turn so tightly that he comes within a hair of swiping the parked cars along the curb. It's a thing of beauty, like automotive ballet.

Eric is impressed.

The driver of the black-and-white tries the same thing, with far less elegant results. The car smashes right into the side of a utility truck and crumples like a beer can smashed with a brick.

❧ ❧ ❧

Harry sees this and immediately panics.

"Don't," Harry says.

But it's too late. Without hesitation, Eric smoothly, and with surprising ease, accomplishes the same move as Wolf, the cop car drifting around the curve, clipping off the driver's side mirror of the crashed cruiser.

"Je-zus!" Harry says.

Eric bites back a smile.

Wolf glances in the rearview mirror as Eric's car comes out of its drift and roars up behind him. Now its his turn to be impressed, the same way a prizefighter might be with an opponent's punch, even as it comes right at his face.

Harry is not. "Are you trying to get us killed?"

"I'm trying to catch the guy in front of us."

"It's the same thing."

That's when Mike's Vespa shoots out in front of them.

Eric slams on the brakes. Mike swerves, his Vespa flipping on its side and sliding across the asphalt.

Harry slams his fist against the dash. "That's it. Pull the fuck over."

"But he's getting away."

"Stop the car now. That's an order."

Eric reluctantly does as he's told and looks ahead as the Audi drifts around another curve and disappears. Harry holds his hand out to Eric.

"Give me the keys."

Eric does, then looks over his shoulder to see how the driver of the Vespa is doing.

❧ ❧ ❧

Mike is fine—his jacket and helmet saved him from getting scratched up—but can't restart the damn Vespa. He glances at his watch. Three minutes left. He's not going to give up. He grabs the pizzas, ditches the Vespa, and runs the rest of the way to Reed's Garage.

He's going as fast as he can, holding the pizzas in front of him with one hand. As he reaches Reed's Garage, he can see Katie standing in the parking lot out front, holding a stopwatch.

Mike runs right up to her and stops, gasping for breath, as she clicks the stopwatch and makes a show of studying the dial.

"One minute, ten seconds late," Katie says. "Thanks for the free pizzas, Mike."

"You wouldn't, would you?"

Before she can answer, a Reed's Garage tow truck arrives carrying Nicole's red Ferrari, followed by a yellow taxi. And coming up behind those two vehicles is a lime-green Toyota Camry. Two mechanics get out of the Camry, laughing so hard it's a wonder they don't lose control of their bladders.

Mike looks at Katie again, and now she's laughing, too. "With all the cars you had on the road, you could have picked up the pizzas yourself."

"But then they wouldn't have been free."

Mike is about to give her hell when he sees something that makes him forget all about pizzas, docked pay, and breathing. Nicole climbs out of the cab, a move that, despite her being fully clothed and engaged in a common action, might as well be a graphic demonstration of a position out of the *Kama Sutra*.

He approaches Nicole while simultaneously admiring her car.

"Nice ride," he says, still holding the pizzas.

"It's my husband's," Nicole says, "and it's junk. It didn't get me where I was going."

"She hasn't been driven in a while." Mike strokes the hood with his free hand and looks Nicole right in the eye.

She meets his gaze. "No, she hasn't."

"That's a tragedy. She's a high-performance vehicle that has to be driven hard and fast," he says. "All the time."

Katie takes the paperwork from the tow truck driver and hurries over to the two of them. "What he means, Mrs. Devereaux, is that when a car sits for a long time, the rubber hoses and seals start to leak, the bearings get rusty, and the fluids go bad."

Nicole answers Katie while holding her gaze on Mike. "I know what he means."

Mike smiles. "It's important to have tight seals and well-lubricated pistons."

"Is it?" Nicole says. "How would you know?"

"I've looked under a few hoods."

It's more than Katie can stand. She glares at Mike and hands him some cash. "Hey, my guys are starving and their pizzas are getting cold. Shouldn't you be serving them some food?"

Mike nods and starts to go. Nicole speaks up. "Thanks for the advice, pizza man."

"Anytime. You have my number." He turns so she can see the big phone number emblazoned on his back. She laughs and so does he as he goes off towards the open garage. Katie clears her throat to get Nicole's attention.

"Most likely it's something simple like old gasoline cut with ethanol clogging up the fuel filter or a weak battery toasted by the LA heat. A Ferrari won't engage the fuel pump if the battery isn't putting out enough volts. Whatever it is, I can have your car ready for you to pick up tomorrow afternoon."

Nicole eyes Katie, as if seeing her for the first time. "You're the mechanic?"

"I'm not wearing this outfit as a fashion statement."

"Of course you are." Nicole gestures to Mike, who has his back to them as he walks into the garage. "But that's not why he is wearing his. By the way ..."

Nicole reaches out and opens two more buttons on Katie's mechanics' jumpsuit to reveal a hint of her cleavage. "He might notice you if you reminded him that you're a woman."

"I don't need to be noticed," Katie says, buttoning her jump-suit back up. "I'll give you a call with an estimate before we do the work."

"Don't bother. Just fix it."

She hands Katie her empty espresso cup, goes to her wait-ing cab, and drives off. Katie tosses the cup in a trash can and marches to the garage.

"Bitch," she mutters.

When she gets inside, Mike is opening up the pizza boxes on a table for the crew and even helps himself to a slice. She takes a slice from the box and feeds it to the pit bull guard dog resting on a cushy car-shaped doggy bed in the corner. His name is Raptor. She turns back to face Mike.

"Do you really think you have a shot with that woman?"

"Why not?" he asks.

"Because she's married and rich. Women like her are social-climbing leaches who only go for men who can take care of them. And you're just a pizza delivery guy."

"So help me change my life," Mike says. "Let me race for you."

"You can't even deliver a pizza on time." She heads over to two cars, a Ford Focus and a Subaru Impreza WRX, that she's transforming into street racers.

Schmitty is working on the Subaru and is covered in grease and surrounded by disorganized carts of equally greasy hand tools.

The Ford is running and being tested by Roger, Katie's fifteen-year-old cousin, who is sitting in the driver's seat studying his MacBook, which is plugged into the engine's electronic control unit. Roger is gangly and looks like he combs his hair with a blender.

"I'm the best," Mike says. "Give me the keys to the Ford and five minutes of your time and I'll take you on a ride that will curl your hair."

Mike flashes his most charming smile, but Katie is immune to it. "I can't. My little cousin is still hacking the custom ECU and calibrating the timing."

"*Little?*" Roger says, sticking his head out of the car. "What do you mean by that?"

"You're younger than me, Roger, that's what I meant. Not everything a woman says is a reflection on your manhood."

Schmitty, Roger, Mike, and every man in the garage answer her in unison, sounding like the Pips. "Yes, it is."

Katie faces them. "Oh, grow up."

Mike sighs. "I prefer the American car, because I'm naturally patriotic, but just this once, I'll lower my standards, expand my worldview, and take the Subaru."

"It has a driver," Katie says.

"Okay, but when that Ford is ready, you're going to need someone to drive it. I'm that guy. Let me prove it to you."

"Are you sure you can handle a vehicle that doesn't have a kickstand?"

Kickstand.

That's when Mike remembers the Vespa he left behind, blocks away.

"Shit!" He abruptly bolts out of the garage, much to Katie's amusement.

She turns to face Roger. "I need that car on the street, winning races. It doesn't make any money while it's in the garage."

"If I get it fixed today, can I race it for you?"

Katie gives him a stern look. "First the pizza guy, now you? You don't even have your license. You're lucky that I let you *park* the car. Your mother would fly back from New Zealand and kill me if she knew I even did that."

"Mom wouldn't come back from her trip unless her fourth husband left her and there was a fifth one here ready to marry her."

"Just fix the car." She goes to her office.

Schmitty moseys over to Roger and motions to the Ford. "Let me tell you something, my boy. Cars are like women. Giving them too much to drink doesn't make them fast and loose. They just get drunk, throw up all over you, and fall asleep afterwards."

Roger thinks about that a moment. "You're saying the air-fuel mixture is too rich, but you're wrong."

"Says who?"

Roger points to the MacBook screen. "Look at the stats. It shows that the timing, fuel pressure, manifold temperature, oil pressure, and RPMs are all perfect. The numbers don't lie."

"Who is the mechanic? You or the computer?"

"I am."

"So start acting like one." Schmitty slams the laptop shut, pulls Roger out of the car, and drags him over to look at the engine. "A true mechanic looks, feels, and listens."

Schmitty leans under the hood, sniffs the air, and listens to the running motor. Then he goes back to the driver's seat, sticks his foot on the accelerator. Black smoke comes out of the tailpipe.

"And what this car is saying by puking up fuel vapor is that it would run a lot better if you'd lean the mixture out." Schmitty takes a screwdriver out of his pocket and hands it to Roger. "Try using my software."

Schmitty walks away. Roger regards the screwdriver for a moment, opens his laptop, and begins tapping the keys with the tool.

"Not bad," Roger says.

CHAPTER TWO

Detectives Eric Visnjic and Harry Prendergast walk into the police station, one of the newest in LA, flat screens and pinpoint halogens everywhere. Horatio Caine would be very comfortable here.

Harry has a newspaper tucked under his arm. "Why don't you get started on writing up the reports."

"What are you going to be doing?"

Harry pauses in front of the men's room door. "I'll be in the library, doing some important reading."

He goes inside. Eric grimaces, knowing that he won't see Harry again for at least another forty-five minutes, and goes into the squad room, resigned to the drudgery ahead of him. He's about to sit down at his unbelievably orderly desk when he spots Detective Donald Neubeck sitting down at his desk with a big Subway sandwich and a supersize Coke, the lunch du jour for most of the detectives. That's because the nearby Subway franchise treats the local cops very well, with a generous law enforcement discount that ensures that there are cops in the place all day, which keeps the vagrants and scumbags away.

Eric takes a deep breath and goes over to Neubeck's desk. "Excuse me, are you leading the investigation into the insurance agency robbery?"

Neubeck looks up at him with a pair of bloodshot eyes that have got a set of bags underneath them large enough to carry groceries. His nose is large and flat, like a balloon that's lost its helium. He's older than Eric but a good decade younger than Harry and is in a constant state of irritation, a man with acid reflux of the soul.

"Right now I'm trying to investigate this sandwich, but I'm being interrupted."

"I'm only asking because I have a vested interest. I was part of the pursuit and I hated to see the guys get away."

Neubeck nods and sets his sandwich down. "You're the rookie who was riding along with Harry."

"Yes, sir."

"I hear that Harry did some pretty spectacular driving today. He's a dinosaur, but he's full of surprises."

Eric hides his irritation with his glory-hungry partner. "He certainly is. Why would anyone want to rob an insurance agency? It's not a cash business."

"It's a front for Willy Stang's money-laundering operation. Stang has been running the gambling racket in the valley since I was a kid at Taft."

"Wouldn't robbing him be suicide?"

"Not if you think you're bigger and badder than he is. I'm guessing that he was hit by a crew working for Gregor Gargolov, a mobster from the Ukraine who's trying to muscle his way into Stang's territory. I hear Gargolov's got two kids at Viewpoint, up on Mulholland. Tuition's got to be forty grand a year."

"Do you think you'll make an arrest?"

"Everyone who was working in the insurance agency fled before we arrived. So we have no victims, no witnesses who actually saw the robbery, and no evidence that it even occurred. What's the point of trying?"

"Because two officers were injured in the pursuit."

"They were barely scratched. It was their car that took the beating. I've got other cases to work on with real victims that I've actually got a shot at closing."

"But what if you *could* close this one?"

"And bring down Stang and maybe Gargolov? I'd probably get bumped up a rank for pulling it off, which should tell you something about what a dead end this one is."

Neubeck picks up his sandwich.

"I'd like to help," Eric says, leaning forward on the desk. "Think of me as extra manpower, day or night. Any grunt work you need, sir, I'm your man."

Neubeck looks up at Eric, brimming with eagerness and ambition, and he suddenly feels very tired. "There is one thing you could do for me that would really push this case forward."

"Yes, sir?"

"Let me finish my goddamn lunch in peace."

Eric tries to hide his disappointment with a firm, respectful nod and goes back to his desk, where he sits with his back to Neubeck.

And that's when it occurs to him that he doesn't need Neubeck's blessing to investigate. He's a detective, too, and he's paid to detect. So that's what he's going to do.

When many of the oil wells of Southern California went dry after seventy years of constant pumping, vast refineries were abandoned almost overnight, most of them left to rot on thousands of acres of arid soil too toxic for even the greediest of developers to subdivide into housing tracts.

Now these sprawling complexes, with their miles of cracked pavement, rusting towers, decrepit buildings, huge oil tanks, massive warehouses, and countless bundles of pipes of all diameters crisscrossing overhead, creating tunnels and bridges of snaking steel, resemble decaying industrial cities in some postapocalyptic future. And that's one way they are used, by directors looking for cool, cheap locations for their dystopian science fiction movies and music videos.

But they also make perfect courses for street racing, with enough obstacles and challenging curves to attract the best drivers, vast enough to draw a large crowd, and remote enough not to attract the police (or, if authorities do arrive, for lookouts stationed at key points to give everyone enough notice to make a quick escape).

It's at one of these refineries tonight, up the coast from Los Angeles in a barren patch of Ventura County surrounded by low hills, where hundreds of people, most of them in their twenties, are watching cars roar between buildings, through warehouses, and around tanks and towers, sometimes barely scraping through the many sudden, narrow bottlenecks in the improvised track, the paved spaces between the structures.

Katie's Impreza is neck and neck in the race with a 2001 Camaro SS. They're drifting around turns and roaring into straightaways, but just when it seems like one of them might be inching ahead, they hit a bottleneck, forcing one of the cars to back off or slam into the side of a building, tower, or tank.

The routes are lined with people, many of them on the catwalks that run all over the refinery, filming the action to livestream with their smartphones.

There's a cracked parking lot that's both the starting line and finish for the race, and it's clogged with great-looking people and their gleaming, pimped-out rides: Japanese imports and American muscle cars pumped up on vehicular steroids, exploding with horsepower, blazing with neon, bursting with amps, and literally spitting fire out of their tailpipes. Nissan 370Zs, 1980s Cutlasses and Monte Carlos, Mazda RX-8s, Subaru WRXs, classic Mustangs and Chargers, Mitsubishi Eclipses, and Chevy S10 pickups, all tricked out, chromed, adorned with decals, and flaunting their metal flesh.

It's a party that's as much of a draw as the race itself, which would be impossible for most of the spectators to see if not for crowd-sourced live-stream, which is played out on smartphones and on multiple large flat screens mounted in the rear of a tricked-out Hummer that's like a rolling multimedia stage.

Katie and Roger are at the Hummer, watching the action, practically pressed up against the monitor by the surging, enthusiastic crowd. For once, she's not in her overalls. She's wearing a scoop-neck T-shirt, a leather jacket, and skinny jeans with black, belted motorcycle boots.

"How much do we have in play on this?" Roger asks.

"Everything I've got left. Five hundred to buy in and then another thousand on bets."

"That's everything? It doesn't seem like much at all."

"Hey, it costs a lot to trick out and maintain our two cars, more than we earn doing tune-ups and oil changes for soccer moms."

"They why do you do it?"

"Anybody can service an engine and rotate tires, but finding the soul of a car and unleashing it, well, that's art. It's also expensive." She takes Roger by the arm and leads him away from the crowd at the Hummer. "The bank is taking the garage away from us if I don't come up with fifty grand in six days."

"Six days!" Roger says. Katie motions at him to lower his voice. When he speaks now, his voice is just loud enough for her to hear over the crowd. "How are you going to do that?"

"By being out here for every race, gambling on our driver. I'm only telling you this because we're family, and to fire you up to get that Ford up and running. If you breathe a word of this to anyone in the garage, I'll beat you to death with your laptop."

"I thought the garage was family," Roger says.

"That's different."

"If it was, you wouldn't be fighting so hard to keep the place. How much can we win today?"

"Four, maybe five thousand. Depends on how much is in the pot."

"And if we lose?"

Her face tightens. There's no way to sugarcoat this. "We lay off all the mechanics and sell the Ford and the Subaru tomorrow."

Elsewhere in the crowd, Wolf is lying on the hood of a yellow 2011 Mustang Shelby GT500, listening to his iPod, while Clem and Axel are watching the race play out on Marcus's iPhone.

"The guy in the Subaru can drive," Marcus says.

"Anybody can drive," Wolf says. "Find me someone who can race."

Mike Cassidy, pizza box in hand, walks up to Reed's Garage. There are several cars parked in the lot and a beat-up Airstream trailer, a light on inside. He creeps up to the trailer and peers in the window.

Schmitty is asleep on the couch in the cramped but cozy trailer, a glass bong and some empty beer cans on the floor beside him. The TV is on, playing a *Monk* rerun. Every flat surface is covered with car magazines and repair manuals.

Mike makes his way to the closed garage, squats down in front of the lock on the office door, sets the pizza box aside, and pulls a lockpick from his jacket pocket. He has the door unlocked in two seconds. He picks up the pizza box and slips inside.

The instant he's inside he finds himself facing the snarling pit bull, which is almost foaming at the mouth with bloodlust. But Mike isn't scared at all. He just smiles, opens the pizza box, and cautiously sets it down in front of the dog.

"Pepperoni, sardines, and extra cheese," Mike whispers. "Just the way you like it, Raptor."

The dog stops snarling and starts gobbling up the pizza. Mike pets the dog on the head and goes to the pegboard filled with keys.

The race at the refinery is coming down to the final stretch. The Trans Am is drifting into a turn so tight that the car sideswipes the building, setting off a shower of sparks. But in that same turn, the Subaru manages to squeeze in, drifting close enough to the Trans Am that it comes within a millimeter of taking off its driver's side mirror.

Time seems to slow down for Shank, the driver of the Trans Am, whose day started off like shit with the robbery and now is going to end even shittier with him losing this race. He tries to see who is driving the Impreza, but the Subaru's window tinting is so dark, all he sees is his own reflection and the look of furious disbelief on his face.

If he didn't need both hands to steer the car, he'd flip off the phantom driver, who now glides his car past Shank to take over the lead, blasting out of the drift and across the finish line.

But whoever the driver is, he doesn't stop to bask in the glory of his win. He just keeps on driving into the night, the crowd cheering in his wake, nobody louder or with more excitement than Roger, who leaps into the air with glee. Katie sighs with relief and seeks out Money Man, a thirtyish guy in a loud, aloha-flowered shirt and wearing so much bling, he makes Flavor Flav, Sammy Davis Jr., and Mr. T seem underaccessorized by comparison. All he needs is a string of lights and he could imper-sonate a Christmas tree.

"Your phantom driver has got to lose one of these days," he says to Katie, handing her a thick wad of cash.

"Wanna bet?"

"Always," Money Man says.

They share a smile and she walks away, taking Roger with her.

It's a half hour later and the crowd is anxious for another race. Money Man can feel it. If he doesn't get some action going soon, the night is going to end early and he'll be out some serious cash.

He approaches Wolf, who is still listening to his iPod and lying on the hood of his Mustang, which is now parked at the starting line. His crew huddles nearby.

"Are you ready to race?" Money Man asks.

Wolf snaps his fingers. Marcus steps up and hands Money Man five hundred dollars in crumpled bills. It looks like a hand-ful of used Kleenex, but Money Man takes it, stuffing it into his pocket, and then turns to the crowd milling around.

"Who wants to take Wolf on?"

Nobody seems willing. In fact, they seem afraid.

"C'mon, did you come here to race your cars or park them?"

Still, nobody comes forward. Money Man can feel his profits evaporating.

"Come on, there's got to be somebody here with some balls."

And then the crowd parts for the arrival of a new player. A sleek red Ferrari California glides up beside Wolf's Mustang. Wolf sits up to see who gets out of the car.

It's Mike.

Wolf shakes his head. "I didn't order a pizza."

His crew laughs. Mike smiles.

"Maybe you should. That way you cowards will have something to eat while you watch the real men race."

The laughter abruptly stops. Wolf slides off the hood of his car and gets right in Mike's face. Mike doesn't flinch, and his good-natured smile doesn't waver.

"It's a five-hundred-dollar buy-in," Wolf says. "You got the cash?"

"Nope. But you'll stake me the money and race me anyway."

"Why would I do that?"

"Because if you don't, it's going to look like you're using money as a lame excuse not to race me. Everybody will know that you're afraid of losing to me, which, if you're smart, you should be."

Wolf nods to Marcus, who takes out another wad of cash and hands it to the Money Man.

"I'm going to need some collateral," Wolf says.

"The car isn't mine," Mike says.

"No shit, delivery boy. If I win, I want your hand."

"I didn't know you liked me that much."

Wolf snaps his fingers. Clem steps forward and shows them the small ax that's behind his back. Mike wasn't expecting that. Nobody was.

Clem grins. "Now let's see who's a coward."

Mike glances at Wolf. "You're not serious."

"Ask Ortega."

"Who's Ortega?"

"That'd be me," says a voice in the crowd.

Mike turns to see a short, sullen Hispanic man stepping forward. There's a bandaged stump where his right hand used to be. Mike glances at Money Man, who nods, confirming that it's true.

"So what are you doing back here?" Mike asks.

"I'm going to race again. Not tonight, but someday."

"You can't win your hand back."

"No, but maybe I can take his," Ortega says, tipping his head towards Wolf.

"Or lose your other hand," Mike says.

Ortega shrugs. "That's the only way I'll ever stop racing."

Mike stares at him, incredulous. Before Mike can say anything, the Trans Am pulls up, the driver's side window rolled down.

"I'll take that bet," Shank says. "Anybody who can't beat a dickhead asshole and a pizza delivery boy deserves to lose their shifting hand."

Wolf looks at Mike. There's a long moment as Wolf moves to the beat of whatever song he's listening to and Mike considers the odds. Mike comes to a decision.

"Okay, I'm in, but if I win, I get the cash, your share of the pot, and your iPod."

Wolf nods. The race is on. The crowd mobs the Money Man, everyone eager to get their bets in.

A woman who looks like she got her boob job done at Walmart stands wearing a laced halter top and a micromini in front of three cars: the Trans Am, the Ferrari, and the Mustang. She's counting down, unlacing her halter top as she does.

"Ready ... set ... go!"

She rips off her halter and flashes her headlights, and the cars speed off, narrowly missing her.

Yeah, using a woman like this is exploitative, sexist, and crude, but that's street racing for you.

And besides, she's gets off on it or she wouldn't do it.

Shank takes an early lead. He drives screaming in a speed-junkie frenzy, fueled by frustration and rage and a very bad fucking day.

Mike drives like he was born with a steering wheel in his hand. It's a fluid, almost supernatural fusion of man and machine. He drives like his personality: reckless, fun loving, cocky.

Wolf doesn't seem engaged in the race at all, more into the music he's listening to than the car he's driving. But that's because the music and the race have a flow, a natural current, and he's riding them both like a surfer on a wave. He twists his wheel and rams against the passenger side of Mike's Ferrari, forcing him onto a loading ramp.

Mike can't turn off the ramp without rolling the car. He's forced to go along with it, speeding up the incline and flying into a warehouse. The Ferrari sails through the air, hits a row of overhead lights, shattering them, then slams hard into the ground, the car spinning out of control before he manages to bring it to a stop an inch away from two immense pillars.

Whew.

He sits for a moment, dazed and astonished at what he's just survived, but then he realizes that there's still a race going on and he's not part of it anymore. He looks at his right hand.

Shit.

Wolf closes in on the Trans Am as they roar down a narrow passage underneath a low canopy of pipes. He thinks back to the police car that was chasing him and what the cop was probably planning to do to him.

A pit maneuver. Clip the car and make it spin out of control. But Wolf has a better idea.

Wolf speeds up and clips the left rear bumper with the edge of his right front bumper.

The Trans Am spins, and in that instant when the driver's side is now tipped directly in front of Wolf, he slams into the car again, rolling it. The car seems to roll forever, disintegrating more and more with each impact.

Wolf drifts around the rolling car, just for show, nothing between him and the finish line now. He's so caught up in his impending victory that he doesn't see the Subaru Impreza parked in the darkness, the motor running.

There is no way out of the warehouse except the way he came in, and he won't win the race doing that. So Mike drives across the warehouse, makes a U-turn, then floors it, driving headlong towards the corrugated metal wall ahead, building up as much speed as he possibly can.

The Ferrari bursts through the wall and flies directly into the path of Wolf's Mustang, cutting him off and taking the lead, dragging bodywork and a sheet of corrugated metal that creates a wake of sparks.

Mike looks over his shoulder and is surprised to see the sparks, the Mustang, and the Trans Am rolling behind him.

The Trans Am finally comes to a halt, crumpled nearly flat. There's no way Shank survived. His body will have to be removed from the car with a vacuum.

Mike charges across the finish line, only a second or two ahead of Wolf, and comes to a screeching, rubber-burning stop. He's won, but the Ferrari is trashed, smoking, knocking, and dragging its front bumper. Not that he gives a damn about the car. The damage is a badge of honor, proof for all to see of what he went through, the death that he cheated, to reach this moment.

He sits there and lets the moment sink in.

His heart is pounding, harder than if he'd run a mile, and he feels light-headed, almost weightless. He removes his hands from the steering wheel. They're shaking from gripping the wheel so hard. Or perhaps it's the adrenaline coursing through his veins. Whatever it is, it's more than relief, or fear, or excitement, or mere pride.

It's the first time he's felt truly alive, aware of his full potential. And in that moment, he knows he has to do this again.

He gets out of the car, nearly tumbles on his weak knees, and then, feeling the eyes of the excited crowd on him, practically swaggers over to collect his cash from the Money Man, who nods with admiration.

"Where did you learn to drive like that?" Money Man asks, handing Mike a stack of cash.

"That was nothing," Mike says. "Just a Sunday drive to church for a Tennessee boy like me. You should see me when I'm trying."

He shoves the money in his shirt pockets and ambles up to Wolf, who launches himself out of his car, seething with rage. He gets right into Mike's face. Mike holds out his right hand, palm up.

"You owe me an iPod," Mike says.

Wolf yanks out his earbuds, pulls the iPod out of his pocket, and slaps it in Mike's hand.

"Thanks. I hope this isn't filled with thirty gigs of Neil Diamond." Mike grins at Wolf, and at his three buddies, and hops back into his Ferrari.

It would be a truly triumphant moment for him, if only he didn't have to stick his head out of the car and ask:

"Could I have a push?"

A bunch of people rush out behind the car and give him a push, and the engine catches, the car sputtering and knocking and puking out smoke as he drives away.

It's late. Katie is testing the engine on the Ford, the hood closed and the wheels rolling in place on the dyno, sort of an automotive treadmill. She's standing in front of the car, her eyes closed, listening to the purr of the engine, swaying to the natural rhythm as the Subaru drives up outside.

The driver emerges from the car, stepping out of the darkness into the light of the garage.

It's Eric Visnjic.

He comes up behind her and wraps his arms around her waist. She melts against him.

Eric nuzzles her neck and begins to unbutton her shirt from behind. He cups her breasts and teases her nipples until they're hard. She moans, resting her head against his chest, and reaches back to grab his ass. She gives his buttocks a hard squeeze.

Katie turns and they kiss. And kiss. And kiss. He lifts her up onto the hood of the Ford. She wraps her legs around him, draws him close, and unbuckles his pants.

There are no words, just the music of the engine.

Before Katie's father died, the space above the garage was used for storage. But when money got tight and they lost the house, she and Stephen converted the space into two small bedrooms and a kitchenette. She hasn't touched Stephen's bedroom. Her room is barely more than a mattress on the floor, a bunch of pillows, and a heavy comforter, which she and Eric are now huddled under.

"I wish you didn't have to sneak around," she says.

"It's already bad enough that Schmitty and Roger know what I'm doing. Street racing is illegal. I could lose my badge if my bosses find out what I do. Or lose my life if the racers believe that I've betrayed them."

"You haven't."

"Yet. Some guys robbed Willie Stang's money-laundering operation this morning."

"Stang has been around forever."

"I think the getaway driver was a street racer."

"How do you know?"

"The way you drive is unique. It's like the way you—"

"Fuck," Katie interrupts.

"I was going to say walk. I saw Wolf use the same moves at the race tonight. I followed him back to a garage owned by Gregor Gargolov, who is muscling in on Stang's territory. If I can arrest Wolf and get him to turn against his boss to save himself, it could make my career."

"What's stopping you?"

"I can't arrest Wolf without revealing to my superiors what led me to him."

"So lie."

"I'm not very good at it."

"That's because you're too straight."

"You didn't seem to mind a few minutes ago."

She tickles him and he squirms away to protect himself, nearly ending up on the floor.

"You won't bend, even a little," she says, "even when it would do you some good."

"I'll just have to find another way to get the same information."

"If you're so afraid of the police finding out that you're a street racer, why do you do it?"

"I grew up in Bosnia during the war. It was anarchy. I never knew what would happen next. I had no control over anything."

"Nobody does," Katie says.

"I never want that kind of uncertainty in my life again. And when I'm behind the wheel of a car, there isn't any. It feels like I'm in control of everything. I experience total calm, true peace. It's like being here with you."

"Because you think you can control me?"

"Because I love you." He rolls over and kisses her. She stiffens and pulls away from him.

"You may not have the Subaru much longer."

The abrupt change of subject is not lost on him. He wisely decides not to make an issue of it. He pinches her playfully. "You don't like the way I drive?"

"I like it very much. But if I can't come up with fifty grand in six days, the bank will foreclose on the garage."

"There are other garages. You'll get another one."

She sits up and glares at him. "How can you say that? There are no other garages, Eric. My mother died when I was three, my father when I was sixteen, my brother when I was nineteen … This garage is the only thing I have left that we all shared. If I lose this, I lose them."

He sits up and puts his hands on her bare shoulders. "Then you won't."

"How can you be sure?"

"Because I will win the next race, and the one after that. And the one after that. Until you have your money."

She looks him in the eye. "You can't know that."

"I promise."

She gives him a deep kiss, pushes him back on the bed, and straddles him. "Let me show you how I drive."

Katie plants her hands on his chest and begins to grind against him. He reaches up and sucks her breast. She moans, jams his cock inside her, and rides him fast and hard. Their excitement is building quickly. But suddenly she stops, tipping her head to one side to listen.

"Do you hear that?"

"It sounds like a car. Keep driving."

"It's a Ferrari with a blown head gasket and a leaking radiator."

"So?" He nuzzles her breasts and clutches her back, trying to urge her on.

"The car didn't have any of those problems yesterday when it was in my garage."

She climbs off Eric, steps into her panties, and grabs a bathrobe.

"Where are you going?" he asks.

She doesn't answer. She just runs out.

"Terrific," Eric says and searches for his pants.

Katie runs barefoot down the stairs into the garage to find Mike standing sheepishly beside Nicole's smashed Ferrari. She marches up to him, takes one look at the wreckage, and hits him with a right hook that practically knocks him on his ass.

She's about to throw another punch to put him down when Eric runs out, barefoot and shirtless, and holds her back.

"Let me go," she yells, fighting against him.

"Are you going to hit him again?"

"No," she says, "I'm going to kill him."

Mike holds up his hands in surrender. "I know this looks bad, but I won the race." He reaches into his shirt and takes out the roll of cash. "I had to take a little for rent, my bar tab, some gambling debts, but the rest is yours. It's just the beginning of what I can earn for us."

Katie swats the cash out of his hand onto the floor.

"That doesn't begin to cover the damage you've done to this car. Fixing it is going to cost me the money we won in the last race … and much, much more."

Eric pushes Katie aside and decks Mike. The blow knocks him back against the Ferrari. He's about to unleash some more whup-ass on Mike when Katie grabs him around the waist from behind.

"Don't," she yells.

"Why not?" Eric says. "You were!"

"But he'll hit *you* back."

"The son of a bitch can try."

Mike rubs his jaw, glances at the Subaru outside, then back at Eric. "You throw a punch the same way you steer a curve. You put too much thought into it."

Eric gets in his face. "And you don't think at all."

Mike is not the least bit intimidated. If anything, he's amused. "That's my edge. That's why I'll kick your ass, right here or on the road. You decide."

"Here and now."

Katie steps between them, pushing them apart. "That's enough. The customer is coming for her car in the morning. What am I supposed to tell her?"

"So the car is a little dinged," Mike says. "You can fix it. It's what you do. This is a garage."

"It was." Katie turns and walks away.

Mike starts after her, but Eric blocks him.

"What your problem?" Mike says. "There's enough road out there for both of us."

"I don't think so."

Mike glances past Eric to see Katie going back up the stairs. "You're afraid if she sees me drive, you'll become a memory."

"I'm afraid you're going to take away the most important thing in her life."

Mike smirks and gives him a once-over. "You? She can do better."

"This garage. She has to pay off the bank in six days or it's gone. You just put her in the hole. If you also put her out of business, I will take you down." Eric steps into his face again. "I may do it anyway."

Mike says nothing. He just turns his back to Eric and walks away. Eric stays where he is until he's sure Mike is gone. Then he goes out to the parking lot, where he's got his Ford F-150 pickup parked. He opens the cab, roots around in a gym bag on the floor, and comes out with what looks like a leather shaving kit.

Eric takes it to the Ferrari, squats in front of the door, and opens his kit, taking out a tin of powder and a brush. He uses the brush to dust the door, raises several sets of fingerprints. He reaches into his bag for a strip of fingerprint tape and begins to lift the prints, which he affixes to strips of paper. When he's done, he takes his iPhone from his bag and photographs each one.

It's early morning. The only one in the detective bureau is Eric, who has his iPhone plugged into his computer, watching the monitor as the print-recognition software analyzes the prints he lifted.

Five faces come up on-screen: four men, two women. He recognizes two of the faces. Nicole Devereaux, the woman he ticketed on Ventura Boulevard, and Mike Cassidy.

Small world.

Eric clicks on Nicole's face and brings up a U.S. immigration form. Nothing there to interest him. He clicks on Mike's face and an arrest record comes up from the Tennessee State Police. He's just beginning to scan the document when he hears footsteps behind him. He quickly clicks out and brings up his Gmail account.

"Browsing porn sites?" Harry asks.

"Checking my email. What did the captain want with you?"

"One of Stang's men was murdered at the old Petro West refinery last night, probably by one of Gregor Gargolov's goons. The Major Crimes Unit is afraid Stang will retaliate and spark a mob war."

Eric thinks about that, and suddenly Wolf's moves in the race last night take on an entirely different meaning. "What does that have to do with us?"

"The department wants as many cops on the street as possible." Harry tosses Eric a set of keys.

"You're letting me drive? After what you did yesterday, I was really hoping to learn some techniques from you."

"You're pissed off I took the credit for your driving yesterday."

"Brilliant deduction," Eric says. "You must be a detective."

"You want to know why I did it?"

"Because you're a shit who wants all the glory?"

"Is that what you call being disciplined for reckless endangerment? That's the glory you would've got if I hadn't told 'em it was me who drove like a maniac yesterday. That's why you get to be on your own in the car today."

Eric winces. The stab of guilt he feels is almost a real, physical pain. "You're being suspended?"

"Of course not. I'm too old to slap down. They just wagged a finger at me, but they would have drop-kicked your ass out of here."

Eric sags with relief. "So why am I driving alone?"

"Because they want a 'highly visible police presence' to discourage Stang or his goons from taking action. That means putting every police car they've got on the road. So it's one officer to a car until further notice. I won't be there to protect you, newbie, so try not to screw up."

Harry walks away. Eric waits until Harry is gone, then brings up Mike's record and prints it out.

At that same moment, Katie, Schmitty, and Roger are in the garage, surveying the damage to Nicole's Ferrari. Mike stands off to one side, looking glum.

Schmitty sighs. "The major body work aside, the exhaust is crushed, the radiator is cracked, and the front right suspension wishbone is bent."

"I was hoping I was wrong," Katie says. "Is there anything that doesn't have to be fixed?"

Roger peers into the car. "The rear view mirror is intact."

"Good, maybe she'll be too busy admiring herself to notice the rest of the damage."

"I don't think so," Schmitty says, and glances behind Katie, who grimaces and turns around slowly to see Nicole standing in the entrance to the garage.

Nicole looks incredible. The flush of anger on her cheeks only adds to her beauty.

"What happened to my husband's car?"

"Me," Mike says, stepping forward. "There was a street race last night. I didn't have a car, so I borrowed yours."

Nicole glares at Katie. "You let him?"

Before Katie can answer, Mike speaks up again. "No, blame me. I took it."

Nicole walks up to him. "Why?"

"I needed the money, but mostly I wanted to prove to Katie what I could do." He looks at Katie, who shakes her head.

"That you could wreck cars?" Katie asks.

"That I'm a damn good driver. You wouldn't give me a chance, so I took one myself," Mike says, then turns back to Nicole. "If you want to call the cops, fine, I'll stick around to be arrested. Otherwise I'll work off the debt by giving you whatever I earn from the races."

Nicole smiles. She likes cocky. "Are you that good?"

"I won last night."

She gestures to the wrecked Ferrari. "This is what it looks like when you win?"

"Look at me," Mike says and meets her gaze as he remembers the pure adrenaline jolt that he felt last night, the mind-blowing rush that comes only from winning and knowing that not only are you are the best at something, but you've given death the finger. Just thinking about it brings back traces of that feeling and, with it, the hunger to experience it again. He smiles at her. "This is what it looks like when you win. A car can be fixed. All it takes is money. You can't buy what I'm feeling."

Nicole tips her head ever so slightly and studies his face, the sparkle in his eyes, the grin. Yes, she can see it. She can even feel it, like a vibration.

"Are these races illegal?"

"Anything that feels this good usually is. Let me show you. Tonight."

She ponders that for a moment, gauges the vibration and what it might feel like jacked up 10,000 percent.

"Okay, pizza man. Show me. Then I'll decide what happens to you." She turns to Katie. "My husband gets back to LA next week. You have until then to make his car look and run like new, or I'll shut you down."

Nicole walks out and gestures with a wave for Mike to follow. He hangs back a moment and flashes a smile at Kate.

"See? Everything will work out."

Katie throws a wrench at him. He ducks out of the way and hurries out after Nicole. Roger shakes his head with admiration.

"He's got the touch," Roger says.

He's right, but Katie is still pissed. She glowers at him. "Go away."

Roger does. Besides, he wants to see Nicole's ride. He runs out into the parking lot in time to catch a glimpse of a Bentley Continental driving away, Mike in the passenger seat.

"The lucky bastard," Roger says.

❧   ❧   ❧

Kathy leads Schmitty into her office and closes the door. "There's something you need to know."

Schmitty nods. "We don't need to worry about her shutting us down because the bank will do it before she does."

"That's the bright side. Today I have to fire all of the mechanics except you and Roger."

He opens his arms and she steps into them for a much-needed fatherly hug. He holds her tight and she rests her head on his chest.

"I have a little money saved up," he says.

"How's that possible on what my father and I have paid you?"

"I don't have a lot of overhead."

"I appreciate it, Schmitty, but keep your money. Whatever you've got wouldn't buy an ashtray for her car."

"The ashtray is one of the few things that we don't have to replace."

They both laugh, as only the truly hopeless can.

CHAPTER THREE

It's not often that one of Sal's employees is dropped off in Bentley to make deliveries on a Vespa, but if there was one thing the pizza chef had learned about Mike over the last few months, it was that the kid was full of surprises.

In fact, that was about the only thing he'd learned about him.

Mike spent the day making deliveries, one after another. There was a lull after the lunch rush, and then Sal got a delivery order for three pies to one of the mansions in the Oaks, the most exclusive of the gated communities in Calabasas.

But as huge as the seventy-five-hundred-square-foot homes are, they're essentially upscale tract homes. The truly exclusive addresses in the Oaks are in the gated community within the gated community. Past that second guardhouse, and the second set of overly ornate gates, were even larger, custom homes, each one an architectural marvel.

As Mike scoots in on his Vespa, he wonders why anyone who could afford a home like this would order out for pizza. But as he nears his delivery destination and sees a familiar yellow 2011 Mustang Shelby GT500 parked on the street, the order makes some sense.

He steers the Vespa up a circular cobblestone driveway (actually, pressed concrete made to look like cobblestones) to a white, two-story, Georgian-style house with ornamental balustrades, a pitched roof, and some Cape Cod flourishes, giving the home a nautical look, though the Santa Monica mountain range stood between the house and any view of the sea. It's a classic example of new money trying to look like old wealth.

Wolf and Marcus are out front, polishing a white Rolls-Royce Ghost, and start laughing as soon as they spot him.

"When did the training wheels come off?" Wolf asks.

"Last night, just before I kicked your ass at the race." Mike takes off his helmet, grabs the pizzas, and saunters up to the guys. "Maybe you boys could shine it for me when you're done with the car."

Wolf drops his rag and advances on Mike. "I'm going to shine my knuckles with your face."

That's when the front door of the house opens and a fit guy in his forties, dressed like he stepped out of an *Esquire* magazine ad for Ralph Lauren casual wear, strolls out, a big grin on his face, tasseled Top-Siders on his feet. The only thing missing from this picture is a sailboat or a few polo players on horses in the background.

"Thank God you're here with those pizzas," Gregor Gargolov says with only the slightest trace of a Russian accent. "Come in, come in."

The man ushers Mike inside and shoots a disapproving look at Wolf and Marcus, who go back to shining the car.

The circular entry hall, with its grand circular staircase, is all dark woods and portraits of countrysides and sailing ships. It sounds like a war is being waged inside the house with heavy artillery.

"You're fast," Gregor says over the sounds of battle.

"There's only one thing in life that I do slowly."

Gregor grins. "Then you haven't smoked a fine Cuban cigar, enjoyed a glass of vintage wine, or savored a gourmet meal."

"Not lately, but they're on my to-do list for the week."

Gregor laughs and leads Mike into an enormous game room with a pool table, pinball machines, and a flat-screen TV the size of a movie theater screen. A half dozen kids, maybe eight or ten years old, are playing World of Warcraft.

"My wife is having her hair done and left me with the kids, who immediately invited their friends over. Now they're starving and all I've got in the house is caviar."

"I hear that a lot in my line of work."

Gregor takes the pizzas from Mike and lays them out on a big table. One of the kids, the chubbiest, notices the food has arrived.

"Pizza!" the kid shrieks.

"They're like piranhas," Gregor says to Mike. "Step back or they'll eat you in their feeding frenzy."

The kids rush up to the table and attack the pizzas. Mike takes a step back.

"You weren't kidding."

Gregor puts his arm around Mike's shoulder and leads him outside. The swimming pool looks like a natural grotto, lined with tropical plants, rocks, and waterfalls. It's beautiful and serene, with an amazing view of the hills. Gregor has set himself up at a table, which is covered with papers and an open MacBook, which he closes as he sits down.

"My name is Gregor Gargolov and you've impressed me."

"Thirty minutes from our door to yours or it's free. That's our motto."

"I'm talking about last night. I'm something of a car-racing fan. I like how you drive."

"Even though I beat your guy?"

"He's not my guy anymore. You are."

"Does he know that?"

"If he's smart, he knew it the moment you passed him."

"Maybe I was just lucky."

"I don't think so. If you drive for me, I'll provide the car, stake your races, and give you ten percent of the winnings."

Mike thinks about that for a moment. "I appreciate the offer, Mr. Gargolov, but I think I'll settle for thirty bucks for the pizzas and a generous tip."

"Do you mind if I ask why? Any other driver would jump at the opportunity."

"I guess I'm not any other driver."

"That much I know." Gregor reluctantly picks up a sheet of paper from the table and holds it up. It's a police sketch of a suspect, one who looks a lot like Mike. "Does he look familiar to you?"

"Chris Hemsworth. Maybe Justin Timberlake."

Gregor rises and approaches him. "Close. This is a police sketch of the wheelman in a failed jewelry store heist in Nashville last year. The robbers tripped a silent alarm. They got caught. But their driver managed to elude a dozen police cars and a helicopter. Quite a feat."

"What happened to him?"

Gregor holds the sketch up beside Mike's head. "Nobody knows, but I have a feeling he fled to California."

The chubby boy comes running outside. "Papa, Herman put his pizza in the DVD player."

"Okay, I'll be right there," Gregor says, then reaches into his pocket and comes out with some cash. "This is parenthood, Mike. One crisis after another. We're already on our fourth DVD player. Can you find your way out?"

"I have a great sense of direction."

Gregor hands him a fifty-dollar bill. "Good, then I know you'll be back to see me again soon."

Nicole is dressed to party and not impressed by the vacant power plant outside Santa Clarita that Mike has dragged her to. It's a sprawling expanse of rusted buildings, holding tanks, and weed-cracked, garbage-strewn asphalt in the middle of nowhere, the muffled sound of music throbbing from deep within the cavernous abandoned building that they're heading for.

"There better be more to this party than a boom box, a pizza, and a couple of beers or you're going to jail," she says.

But Mike just grins and opens the door, ushering her in. She steps inside and it's like passing through a portal into another dimension, one where the air itself is crackling with electricity. There must be three hundred people here, all rocking out to something, whether it's the music, the cars, the drugs, or the sexual energy that is giving the air its snap.

People are dancing and strutting, displaying their flesh and their moves. Cars are everywhere, sparkling with their hoods and doors open, showing off their stuff, or speeding around, weaving among pillars, spinning in circles, or just roaring their exhausts like raging lions declaring their superiority and staking their turf. Everyone is high on something and looking to score—for some it's drugs, for others its sex, for guys like Mike, it's speed.

Nicole is immediately enthralled by it all. "How often does this happen?"

"Every night, somewhere in LA," Mike says, leading her through the crowd.

"And the police don't notice?"

"We stick to the outskirts, keep moving, and watch our backs. A rat couldn't come within a mile of this place without everybody knowing about it."

There's a roar of excitement from the crowd as Katie's Subaru Impreza speeds into the building and drifts along the wide swath that passes for an automotive catwalk, leading to the starting line of the race.

Mike stares into the tinted glass, seething with jealousy and resentment. Nicole notices it, too, and snaps her fingers in front of his eyes.

"Show me more," she says.

Katie approaches the driver's side window of the Subaru. The driver rolls it down a crack so only she can see him.

"What have you bet?" Eric asks.

"The keys to this car. It covered the buy-in and twenty thousand on the line."

Eric glances over at the other cars lined up to race, all of them facing four wide-open loading bays leading out into narrow corridors of asphalt between structures outside. He knows that beyond it is the dark labyrinth of buildings, pipes, and structures that lay between them and the vast, empty spill basin that's the finish line.

Eric isn't worried about the lay of the land. It's the drivers who matter.

"Do you know anything about the guys I'm up against?"

Katie gestures to a BMW M3 that looks like a stockbroker's ride and a white Honda S2000 that's bouncing at the starting line.

"The driver of the white Honda likes to ignite his nitrous on the stretches, so watch out for the afterburn."

"The speed demons don't worry me. Races are won in the turns."

"The Bimmer might not look like much, but I listened to the engine. That's not a stock M3. My guess is they've gutted the car so it's lighter than a Corolla and put in quick-cooling, sequential turbos to give her a real boost."

"It's not the car that counts. It's the person who's driving it."

"It's a woman. Twenty-four years old and very cocky. Word is she's an American Le Mans pro looking to make a quick score off amateurs."

"Then she's in for a shock."

Katie gives him a smile. "You sound confident, Racer X."

"I keep my promises." He smiles back at her and closes the window.

She steps out of the way and gives a nod to Money Man, who sends out a woman in a shiny black skintight latex minidress, slit from the neck down nearly to the crotch, black gloves, and black knee-high boots.

The woman is carrying a whip, of course.

Katie rolls her eyes. The races attract all kinds.

The dominatrix steps in front of the three cars and raises her whip in the air.

"Ready. Set ... *go!*"

She cracks the whip.

The cars speed past her. She screams with almost carnal delight. The race is on.

Mike takes Nicole's hand and leads her to a pimped-out Escalade truck, a huge flat-screen monitor and enormous speakers mounted in the bed. The monitor shows various live-streamed angles of the race, taken from cameras placed throughout the property.

"What are the rules?" Nicole asks, watching the screen as the cars speed, drift, and careen through what amounts to a pitch-black obstacle course in an industrial wasteland.

"Just one. Don't lose."

Nicole squeezes his hand and he looks at her. She is staring at the screen. She is caught up in the magical, erotic allure of this secret world she never knew existed, just as Mike knew she would be.

"Can anybody do it?" she asks.

"If you've got the right car and the five-hundred-dollar minimum buy-in."

"What's the prize?" Nicole asks.

"Your opponent's buy-in and anything else of value that he's willing to lay on the other side of the finish line. But most of us would do it for nothing if the cars didn't cost so much to trick out."

"So how can you afford it?"

"Most of us can't. We've got to find someone like Katie, drive their cars, and take a percentage of what they earn betting on us."

"But it was my car you were driving last night," Nicole says. "What did you have to wager then?"

He holds up his right hand and mimes cutting it off with the edge of his left. She stares at him, not in horror, but in something almost akin to arousal.

"Your hand?"

He nods.

"Unreal. It's worth that much to feel what you do behind the wheel?"

"More," he says.

The Honda spits nitrous fire, roaring ahead of Eric and the BMW in a straightaway. But Eric isn't worried. He scouted this location weeks ago, knowing that someday it would be picked for a race. He knows what's ahead, a bundle of pipes cutting low across a straightaway.

Eric makes a hard turn, drifting across the BMW's path, just as the Honda hits the pipes, shearing off the top of the car like a strip of aluminum foil off a frozen dinner.

The Honda spins out of control and slams into a post, bouncing off it like pinball, narrowing missing the BMW, which speeds past into a bottleneck ahead.

Nicole points to the screen. "I want to drive like that."

"Stick to watching. It's exciting and a lot less dangerous."

"But it doesn't feel as good as doing it."

"How would you know? You've never done it."

"That's true of any virgin, but that only makes the desire to experience it more intense," she says.

"It's not as easy as it looks."

"So teach me," she says. "Show me your moves, pizza man."

He smiles at her. "Will that get me off the hook with you?"

"Or catch you on a different one," she says.

Eric and the BMW are neck and neck, coming into a tight turn. Just as he's about to execute a drift, a wrench flies out of the driver's side window of the BMW and slams into his windshield, shattering it.

He reflexively flinches and jerks the wheel. It's little more than a twitch, but this is precision driving and that's all it takes for him to lose control of the car as he enters the drift. The Subaru slides across the asphalt and one of his tires shreds, exploding like a grenade, strips of smoking rubber flying.

His car slams sideways into a wall.

He can't see a thing out of his window but he doesn't have to. He knows the BMW has crossed the finish line and that he's lost ... both the race and Katie's garage.

Katie is in the crowd watching the monitors. She can't believe what she has just seen.

Money Man saunters over to her. He's wearing so much bling he sounds like he's wearing jingle bells. He holds his hand out to her. She drops a pink slip in his hand.

"I hope it's in one piece," he says. "I'd rather not put any money into it before I sell it."

She flips him off and walks away without looking back. But before she is swallowed up in the crowd, Mike gets a look at her and sees the tears running down her defiant face.

Mike turns to Nicole, who is watching the screen and has no idea of the significance of what has just happened.

"If you really want to learn," he says. "You're going to need a car."

"I've got one," she says.

"Not for this."

Eric slips away from the car before anyone can get a look at him and disappears into the darkness.

He has a long walk back to a street, someplace where he can call a taxi to come get him. He'd driven there in Katie's Subaru, and it never occurred to him that he wouldn't be driving back in it.

He doesn't know how he can face Katie again … or what he could possibly say to her to that could ever make things right.

The garage is dark, as still and silent as a corpse, as Eric emerges from the taxi and walks across the parking lot. He is filled with dread, a man walking to his own execution.

He uses his key to open the office door. The dog looks up at him and wags his tail. They are old friends.

Eric starts slowly up the stairs to Katie's apartment. But as he nears her door, which is ajar, he hears something. Bedsprings creaking to a steadily increasing rhythm. A man's heavy breathing. A woman's moans. The sounds mask the creaking of the steps under Eric's feet as he approaches the door and peers through the crack.

Katie is naked and straddling a man, the muscles in her back straining, her flesh dappled with sweat. She is riding him, moving against him faster and harder, as if she was not chasing a climax but running from a predator. She leans forward, offering her breasts to her lover.

The man rises up, hungrily mashing his face against her breasts, devouring them in his ecstasy.

It's Warren, the banker, losing himself in her bosom, in her, in his lifelong fantasy finally coming true. He cries out as he climaxes.

But Katie is still running, pushing him down with her hands against his pale, scrawny chest, her eyes pinched tightly closed, when suddenly she stiffens, as if felled by a bullet, gritting her teeth against an orgasm that feels more like pain than pleasure.

Eric slips away long before she finally, sadly, looks over her shoulder at the door she left ajar.

It's 7:30 a.m. sharp, and Schmitty and Roger are already hard at work on Nicole's Ferrari. Roger is handing Schmitty tools the way a nurse assists a surgeon as Katie comes down the stairs, weary and unhappy.

"How's it coming?" she asks.

"We're going to need more parts," Schmitty says, "but our credit isn't good anymore with our suppliers."

"We'll pay cash."

"Where's it going to come from?" Roger asks.

"I'll sell the Ford."

Roger is mortified. "You can't."

"We don't have any choice."

Katie walks away. She doesn't have the energy to argue with Roger about the inevitable. She glances outside just as Nicole's Bentley Continental drives up. Katie wasn't expecting to see her yet.

And she certainly wasn't expecting to see Mike ever again, but there he is, getting out of the car with her.

Katie goes outside to meet them. "We still have a week, Mrs. Devereaux."

"It's Nicole, and you can set that job aside for now. I'm giving you a new priority. I want you to get me a street-racing car."

"I just happen to have one that I can sell you."

Mike steps up. "Tell me you're not talking about the Ford."

"It's a great car," Katie says.

"Damn right it is," Roger says, standing in the entry to the garage. "That's why you can't let it go."

Katie turns and glares at him. "You have work to do. Go do it."

"You can keep your car," Nicole says. "I'm not interested in anyone's hand-me-downs. I only buy new. I want you to build me a car."

"I don't make toys for bored trophy wives," Katie says. "I make cars for serious racers."

She turns to go back to the garage, but Mike grabs her by the arm and pulls her around the face him.

"You'll be making hot dogs for a living if you don't get some serious cash right now," he says.

"What do you care how I use the car?" Nicole says. "Make me the ultimate modified street racer and take out your anger at me by inflating the costs. I don't care what it costs as log as it melts asphalt."

Katie yanks her arm free from Mike's grasp. "I'll think about it."

"You'll do it, because this is what you love and you don't have any choice." Nicole opens her purse, takes out an envelope stuffed with cash, and hands it to her. "This should get you started. Call me when it's done."

Nicole goes back to her car, leaving Mike and Katie alone. Mike smiles at her. "Now you're supposed to say, 'Thank you, Mike, for saving my ass," and ask me to race the Ford tonight so you can gamble Nicole's money on me."

Katie's expression hardens into stone. "Get out. Don't ever come back."

"That's not quite as appreciative as I'd hoped," he says, trying to be charming, but it doesn't work with her. She is too damn mad. "I can win races for you, and you need me now more than you did before."

"I'll build her that car, but I don't want to see you at this garage again, not even to deliver a pizza. Do you understand me?"

"Fine."

He turns and gets into Nicole's car. Katie watches them drive off. Schmitty steps up beside her.

"You were awfully hard on him. All he wants to do is drive. I hear he's good."

"He's reckless, irresponsible, and dangerous," she says.

"So is every racer you know."

"Only the ones who've died."

"He's not Stephen," Schmitty says.

"Close enough. I'm done with him. We've got a car to fix and another to build. And only three days left to do both if we want to keep this garage. Let's get to it."

"And the Ford?"

"We'll keep it," she says. "For now."

CHAPTER FOUR

Rich people, celebrities, and mobsters move into gated communities for the tight security. But there's a gaping hole in the security at most of these places. The guards will let in FedEx, UPS, and anybody delivering a pizza warmer with just a wave and smile, no pass necessary.

That's how Mike is able to get past the guards and show up at the front door to Gregor Gargolov's house. Gargolov is lucky Mike isn't a hit man from Willie Stang's organization, or Mike might have blasted through the door with guns blazing instead of politely knocking to announce his arrival.

Wolf opens the door and isn't too pleased to see who is standing there.

"I'm here to see Mr. Gargolov," Mike says.

"Why would he want to see you?"

"We have business to discuss."

"You're too late. He's already hired someone to clean up the dog shit on the lawn."

"You must have been crushed not to get the promotion."

Wolf is tensing up for a fight when Gargolov walks up behind him, a broad smile on his face and wearing an apron.

"Mike, it's good to see you. Come in."

Wolf reluctantly steps aside and lets Mike pass. Gregor leads him into the kitchen, where he's making pasta sauce. He goes back to the stove and stirs the pot.

"What can I do for you?" Gregor asks.

"It's the other way around. I'll race for you."

Wolf's eyes widen in surprise. This is big news for him, since that's his job.

"I am so pleased," Gregor says. "We're going to make a lot of money together and have some fun, too."

Wolf speaks up. "But I'm your driver."

"You still are. You'll be dropping the kids off at school and taking my wife to do her shopping. Give Mike the keys to the Mustang."

"He can keep them," Mike says. "I don't take anyone's hand-me-downs."

Gregor stops stirring. "Is that so?"

"If I'm going to drive for you, Mr. Gargolov, I'll need a car built to my specifications."

Gregor grins, amused by Mike's swagger. "Very well, let's go to my garage and talk to my mechanic." Gregor takes off his apron and tosses it to Wolf. "Don't let the sauce burn."

The telephoto lens on Eric's camera is so good that even from his spot on a fire road on the hillside across the canyon from Gargolov's house, he can see the fury in Wolf's eyes.

Eric can sympathize. He doesn't like Mike much, either, especially now that he knows that he's a car thief, a wanted man, and one of Gargolov goon's.

Eric's iPhone rings. He sets down his camera and glances at the caller ID on the screen. It's Katie. He rejects the call and tosses the phone on the passenger seat. The only positive thing about what he saw last night is that his disappointment in himself is matched by his disgust for Katie.

Unfortunately for him, that doesn't make any of it hurt any less.

Over the next two days, Eric spends every waking hour, which is nearly all forty-eight of them, following Wolf and Marcus, who appear to be staking out a real estate office in Woodland Hills in a silver Audi A6.

A real estate office doesn't strike Eric as hot robbery target, but neither did the insurance agency. So he sticks around the real estate office even after Wolf and Marcus have left to see what makes the place so interesting to Gregor Gargolov ... and ignores a dozen more calls from Katie.

She makes the calls while working 24/7 with Schmitty and Roger, stripping a blue Chevy Corvette C6 Z06 down to its bolts, completely gutting the interior, removing the hood, the bumpers, the air-conditioning, and the engine .... tricking the car out with a roll cage, new turbochargers, a carbon-fiber hood, a 100-shot nitrous system, intercoolers, and much, much more. She won't admit it, but she's thankful to Nicole for this. She loves transforming cars, and being able to spend buckets of someone else's money takes her mind off not having any of her own.

Mike spends his two days much the same way as Katie, practically living at Gargolov's high-tech, ultraclean garage in a business park in Thousand Oaks, overseeing the work of the team of mechanics transforming an already blazingly fast, black Nissan GTR, an all-wheel-drive with a turbo six-cylinder engine, into a jet-black, street-racing monster.

When the two days are over, Eric has a trove of surveillance photos and a pretty good idea of what Gregor Gargolov is planning, Katie has created her best street-racing car ever, and Mike nearly has his dream machine, a gift that he knows comes with strings attached that are drenched in blood.

It's a bright, sunny day in the valley, which, for once, isn't under a thick blanket of smog.

Katie is doing what she likes best, standing alone in front of the finished street-racing car, its engine running. Her eyes are closed. She's not just listening to the Corvette. She's feeling its rumble, sensing its soul.

It takes her a minute to realize that she's not alone, that someone is watching her from behind. At first she thinks it might be Eric, and that soon he'll step up and hold her close to him as if nothing has changed.

But it's not Eric. She can tell from the footsteps, but mostly from the smell of expensive perfume.

It's Nicole, coming to see her new toy. "You're listening to that engine as if it's a symphony."

"Every car sounds different. There's the leopard purr of a BMW, the volcanic rumble of a big-block Chevy, the throaty rasp of an RX-8 … but a car you build yourself from custom parts is even more unique. I want to remember this one." Katie opens her eyes and looks at Nicole, who is now standing beside her. "You wouldn't understand."

"Onomatopoeia."

"What?"

"It's the word for sounds that evoke the image of whatever created them," Nicole says, pleased by the surprise on Katie's face. "I'm not just rich and beautiful. I have an education. One more reason for you to hate me."

She smiles at Katie, who, despite herself, can't help but smile back. Perhaps Katie has underestimated Nicole, who gestures to the car.

"How does it sound?"

"Like rolling thunder. Let me show you where your money went." Katie walks around the car, accompanied by Nicole, as she explains what she's done. "We got rid of the carpet, insulation, window motors, air-conditioning, basically everything that makes a car quiet, comfortable, and that slows it down. We lipo'd nearly one thousand pounds off this baby. We supersized the V-mount components, so both the turbo and intercooler are sweeter."

"Cool."

Nicole has no idea what Katie is talking about and doesn't care, because it's clear that the mechanic not only knows what she's doing but is passionate about it. Katie points to the wheels.

"To slow you down, there are six pot calipers up front and four pot on the rear with drilled rotors. Those are custom rims, of course."

"Of course."

Katie lifts the scissor door on the driver's side, which elicits a giggle of delight from Nicole.

"Scissor doors, they open up over your head or sideways. Completely pointless, but I thought you'd like them."

"I do," Nicole says, squatting down to look at the roll cage and racing seats. The dashboard has been modified to include a bunch of new dials and a custom tachometer.

"We gutted the interior and added bucket seats, new gauges, and nitrous bottles. Push that red button on the dash and this car will blast past anything on the road."

Nicole nods with approval and straightens up. "I'd like to keep the car here. I'll pay you rent."

Katie shrugs. "It's your money. Speaking of which …"

She motions to Nicole to follow her into the office.

As they enter, Nicole notices the wall of family photos. So much love. And in each of the pictures, the garage is as much a part of the family as the people.

Katie hands her an invoice. "Here's your bill. All the parts are listed."

Nicole glances at the bill, then at Katie. "You didn't take enough for labor."

"I took what was fair."

"It won't save your garage. I could write you a check now that would solve all of your problems."

"I'd just be trading one debt for another, and I don't want to be in debt to you."

"You should loosen up." Nicole reaches out and unbuttons the top two buttons of Katie's jumpsuit. "Life would be a whole lot easier."

It's not a pass. There's nothing sexual about it. It's something else. That's when Katie hears the sound of a Vespa driving into the garage. Katie marches out of her office just as Mike steps off the scooter, holding a pizza. He taps his watch.

"Five minutes to spare."

Katie glares at him. "What are you doing here?"

"Bringing you the pizzas you ordered."

"I didn't order any."

"I did," Nicole says, opening the box and taking out a slice, biting into it. "I'm hungry and I'm ready for my driving lesson."

"What are we driving?"

She takes another bite and tips her head toward the Corvette. Mike follows her gaze and it's love at first sight. He hands the pizza box to Katie and approaches the car.

"Sweet."

Mike slides into the driver's seat and closes the door. Nicole tosses her half-eaten slice back into the box in Katie's hands and gets into the car beside him.

"Where do we start?" Nicole asks.

Mike reaches up, rips off the rearview mirror, and tosses it out the passenger window at Katie's feet. "First rule of racing. Never look back. What's behind you doesn't matter."

"What if it catches up?"

"That's what the gas pedal is for." He revs the engine and nods approvingly at what he hears. He smiles at Katie. "Enjoy your lunch."

And with that, Mike drives off. Katie watches them go, then drops the pizza in the trash. She picks up the rearview mirror off the floor and looks at her reflection. She starts to button up her top, then stops, takes another look at her reflection, and reconsiders. Maybe Nicole is right. She unbuttons it again and goes one button farther, showing a hint of cleavage.

Katie sets the mirror down on a worktable, picks up her grease-smudged iPhone, and calls Eric. It rings and rings. She gives up, shoves the phone in her pocket, and storms out of the garage.

She's had enough of his shit.

Mike takes Nicole to the refinery where he trashed her Ferrari. It's totally deserted, except for a few rats.

He enters the facility at high speed, charging around the buildings for a while, seeing what the car can do, and then spots a beer bottle in the middle of the parking lot. He heads for it, then drifts sideways around it, again and again, in a tight circle, making Nicole giggle like a child in a Tilt-A-Whirl at the county fair.

"It's all about throttle control, braking, and steering," he says.

Mike breaks out of the drift into a straightaway without slowing down at all. Nicole points to the red button.

"What happens if I push this?"

"Do it."

She does. The rush of nitrous into the engine gives them an enormous burst of speed that pins them to their seats. The car shoots forwards, the whole world blurring around them. She shrieks with gleeful abandon.

"Speed will get you ahead, but that isn't what wins races. It's steering and psychology, hitting the turns early, taking the inside, and squeezing past your opponent," Mike says as the car slows and he drifts sharply around a turn, barely missing the edge of a building. "Or making it impossible for him to pass you."

He brings the Corvette to a screeching stop, burning rubber. He looks at her. She's breathing hard, her cheeks flushed with excitement.

"Now it's your turn," he says with a smile.

Detective Neubeck is at his desk, going through a stack of files, when Eric approaches carrying two files of his own. That's the last thing Neubeck wants to see, an overeager newbie and even more files.

"How's the Stang investigation going?" Eric asks.

"It's not."

"It is now," Eric says, opens one of his files, and drops a surveillance photograph of the real estate office on Neubeck's desk. "This is the real estate office where Stang has moved his money-laundering operation."

"How do you know?"

Eric hands him photos of people coming and going from the office. "The same people show up every day with heavy gym bags, but when they come out again twenty minutes later, the bags are empty."

Neubeck squints at the photos. "It doesn't mean the bags were full of cash. Maybe they're selling office supplies."

"So why was this guy watching the place, too?"

Eric shows him a photo of Wolf, sitting in a silver Audi.

"Is this guy supposed to mean something to me?"

"He's the getaway driver that we chased."

Neubeck leans back in his chair, which creaks under the strain. "What were you doing watching this place to begin with?"

"I cruised Stang's neighborhood looking for cars that I saw parked around the insurance office the day of the robbery."

"Wait a minute. You actually went back to the insurance office after the chase and wrote down the license plate numbers of the cars that were parked there? Why would you do that?"

"I'm a detective. It's what we do."

"Really? I didn't know that."

Eric ignores Neubeck's sarcasm and goes on. "I ran the plates, nobody had a record, but get this: they all were certified accountants. Either they were auditing the insurance company and, coincidentally, are now auditing the real estate office, or the two businesses have the same employees, whose job it is to count money. And now the same guys who robbed the insurance office are staking this place out. I think Gargolov is preparing to hit Stang again. If they are, we could be there waiting when they rob the place. We can arrest them all and deal a blow to two mobsters at once."

"We could." Neubeck regards Eric in a whole new light. Maybe this kid has some talent after all. The older detective gathers up the photos. "Let me look into this. If you're on to something, I'll see if I can get authorization to put together a strike team for around-the-clock surveillance."

"I'd like to be part of that team."

"I'll see what I can do."

"There's more," Eric says, and opens up the folder on Mike Cassidy and is about to make his case for arresting the son of a bitch, when the senior detective looks past him to the squad room.

"You've got a visitor."

Eric turns to see Harry Prendergast standing beside Katie, whom he's apparently escorted into the building. Both of them are facing him. She's wearing the same outfit she wore to the race, and every guy in the room is looking at her.

"Excuse me for a moment," Eric says to Neubeck. He closes the file on Mike, sticks it under his arm, and hurries over to Katie.

Harvey smiles at him. "You didn't tell me you had a girlfriend."

"I don't." Eric grabs Katie by the arm and leads her into an interrogation room, closing the door behind them. "What are you doing here?"

"You haven't come by, you haven't answered your phone, so here I am."

"What do you want?"

"To give you these." She holds out a set of car keys. "I don't blame you for losing the race, Eric."

"Then I guess there must be another reason you were fucking someone else two hours later. Give the keys to him."

"Warren isn't a racer. He's a banker."

"I hope he gave you an extension on the loan, or it was a wasted fuck."

She slaps him across the face. It's a hell of a smack, almost hard enough to be a punch. He drops the file under his arm, spilling pictures of Mike on the floor.

"I guess he didn't," Eric says.

He's right.

But Katie isn't listening. Her attention is on the mess on the floor, the photos of Mike and printouts of his arrest record. She looks up accusingly at Eric.

"You're following Mike?"

"It's my job. I think he's a fugitive, and if he is, I'm going to arrest him."

"You can't."

"What do I have to lose?"

"What you love."

"I've already lost it."

"I was talking about racing," Katie says.

"I know what you were talking about."

She meets his gaze. "I never said that I loved you."

"You never said that you didn't."

She sighs. "I can't be emotionally involved with a street racer."

"But you could be with someone else."

"Someone else isn't going to die on a hairpin turn."

Eric steps close to her. "Someone else is more likely to than I am."

"I want you back, Eric."

"In your bed and in your car, " he says, "just not in your life."

"That's the way it's always been."

"I don't believe that," he says.

"Believe whatever you want," Katie says. "But you need to race, there's one tonight, and you don't have a car. I've got one for you."

She drops the keys on the floor and walks out of the room, slamming the door behind her. Eric gathers up the photos, organizes the file on Mike again, and then hesitates before picking up the keys.

He puts them in his pocket and goes back into the squad room, heading for Neubeck's desk, but the senior detective is gone. Nailing Mike will have to wait.

But not for long.

Mike is in the passenger seat as Nicole drives, weaving around cardboard boxes that he's set up in the parking lot of the refinery. She keeps flattening boxes with her clumsy turns.

"Control the throttle," he says. "And steer against the turn."

She takes his advice and just clips the box, sending it skittering across the pavement. Mike pulls the hand brake and holds it as she heads into the next turn.

"Steer into it," he says.

She does, and the car makes a perfect, supertight turn. Nicole shrieks with delight. Mike smiles with encouragement.

"Very good. Now let's try a drift around the corner of that building."

"I'll hit the wall."

"I'll talk you through it. Do exactly what I say when I say it."

She nods, heading into the turn.

"Punch the gas and pop the clutch!"

She does, and the car does an uneven drift, barely missing the wall. He points to the turn around the next corner of the building.

"Again," he says.

He gives her the same instruction as before, and the car does another wobbly drift. But it's better. He gestures to the next corner.

"Bang the clutch when you're in the next turn."

She does … shifting gears, turning the wheel, and yanking the hand brake. The car slides smooth and fast around the corner, Nicole in complete control.

Nicole comes to a stop, breathing hard. She unbuckles her belt and turns to Mike. "That was great. What was that?"

"A perfect drift. How did it feel?"

She climbs out of her seat, straddles him, and gives him a deep, passionate kiss. "You tell me."

"Punch the gas and pop the clutch."

She gives him a kiss, even more voracious this time, and grinds her pelvis against him. He runs his hands up her back and presses her closer. She comes up for air and leans back.

"I love my husband."

"I don't care."

"Good." She pulls off her shirt. Her breasts are perfect, her skin flushed, her nipples hard enough to cut glass.

They kiss like they need each other's breath to survive.

CHAPTER FIVE

E ric is at his desk, staring at the keys that Katie gave him, his desire for speed fighting with the pain of betrayal for ownership of his soul, when Neubeck approaches.

"We're on, Visnjic. We got the go-ahead for twenty-four-hour surveillance, starting tonight. Are you in?"

Now he has a third option.

"Absolutely." Eric sweeps the keys to Katie's car into his desk drawer, slams it shut, and walks away with Neubeck.

Fuck the race. He's a cop. He's got a job to do.

Roger is family, so he shares some of the same DNA as Katie. He's also happiest when he's alone late at night with a car, its engine running. But unlike Katie, he doesn't listen with his ears. He uses his laptop.

He's in the front seat of the Ford, the MacBook open on the passenger seat beside him, reviewing the car's performance, when Katie comes up and peers in the window.

"It's ready," Roger says. "All the stats are perfect."

"That's great. Now you can get back to work on Nicole's Ferrari."

"Are you kidding? I'm not missing the race tonight. I want to see this car in action for the first time."

"We're not going. We don't have a driver."

"What about Eric?"

"If he was coming, he would have been here by now."

Roger shakes his head. "We can't sit this one out, Katie. We only have one day left and the bank takes it all."

"That's why tomorrow morning we're selling the car."

Roger's shoulders slump with disappointment. "Could I at least take it once around the block?"

She smiles and gives him a little nod.

"Take it twice, just don't scratch it."

At about that same moment, Mike drives the Corvette to the curb in front of a high-rise apartment tower on Wilshire Boulevard in West Los Angeles. His hair is a mess and his shirt is misbuttoned. He looks like he's been through a wind tunnel. Nicole looks perfect. He peers up at the sleek contemporary building. A broom closet probably goes for a million bucks.

"Which apartment is yours?"

"The penthouse," she says.

"Figures. I'd like to see it."

She shakes her head. "You can have me, but you can't have that."

"I don't want to move in with you," he says. "I just want to see how you live."

"You already do." She gestures to the building. "But that part of my life belongs to Antoine."

"You're afraid people are going to see me and that you'll get caught cheating?"

"He knows about my needs."

"So why isn't he taking care of them?"

"He does, in his way. He lets me have a life separate from his own and doesn't ask questions."

"Do you?"

"Neither one of us expects the other to be faithful, as long as we continue to love each other. We are attached but we are free."

Wow. This sounds way too good to be true. Mike has never heard of a relationship like this. "What about the money you spent on this car?"

"He doesn't care. I can spend what he gives me any way I want. He doesn't ask for an accounting."

"Great. I could use a hundred grand, if he won't miss it."

Nicole laughs. "I am supposed to use the money on things that make me happy."

He gives her his most mischievous smile. "It wouldn't make you happy to give me a hundred grand?"

"Do you really want me to buy you? Would you be happy feeling like my property?"

He shrugs. "That's not what it would be."

"How do you know?"

"Because Antoine bought you and you're happy." Her expression hardens into stone. He's hurt her, and he didn't mean to. "I'm sorry, it was a stupid thing to say. I didn't mean it."

"If you have a problem with this, say it now."

"I don't. Honest."

She turns and looks him in the eye. "My life is too safe, too secure. All the edges are dulled. I need that edge back, to feel my heart beat like it's going to explode, to be part of something besides this marriage. I think I've found it. But I will never leave him, not for anyone or anything."

"I won't ask you to."

"Smart man." She smiles and gives him a kiss that would make most men spontaneously combust. But Mike maintains his cool. She gets out. He watches her go into the building and then drives off, knowing he's the luckiest man in Los Angeles.

Mike is driving the Corvette into the parking lot of Reed's Garage when Katie bolts out, running right across his path. He slams on the brakes to avoid hitting her, but she keeps on going, straight to Schmitty's trailer, and pounds on the door.

Schmitty answers, a bit stoned. "What's wrong?"

"Roger took the Ford and hasn't come back."

That sobers Schmitty up fast. "You didn't tell him you were going to sell it, did you?"

"Yes."

"Shit." Schmitty reaches into the trailer and grabs his leather jacket, which looks like it has been through two world wars, a forest fire, and a tree shredder, and heads for his Harley, Katie trailing after him.

"Wait, Katie." Mike steps out of the Corvette. "I can get you to the race faster than Schmitty can."

"Go with him," Schmitty says. "I'll catch up."

She hesitates for an instant, but her concern for Roger is greater than her dislike for Mike.

Katie gets into the car. He's never seen her look so vulnerable, so scared. "Drive like there's money riding on it."

"It's much more than money," he says.

There are one hundred and sixteen possible moving violations in the vehicle code in the state of California and Mike notches every one of them getting to the abandoned jet engine factory complex in Sylmar.

But he arrives just as the crowd is dispersing, cars peeling off in all directions. One of the cars speeding away is Wolf's distinctive yellow Mustang. The race is over. They drive around the perimeter of the massive plant to find Katie's Ford, smoking and smashed up against a wall, crumpled on all sides from sideswipes and collisions. There's a half dozen people huddled around someone on the ground.

Katie catches her breath. "Oh God, no ..."

Mike comes to a hard stop and Katie runs out. As she breaks through the crowd, he notices something on the hood of the Ford ...

A big bloodstain.

And a severed hand.

Fucking Wolf.

He's still staring at the hand when Katie's wail of despair grabs his attention. He breaks through the crowd to her side and sees Roger on the ground, a crude tourniquet tied around his arm, Money Man pressing a bloodied rag against the raw stump. Roger is pale, his eyes vacant.

Mike looks around and spots an ice bucket full of beers. He smacks Money Man on the back. "Put him in my car. Now!"

Mike tosses the beer bottles out of the bucket and carries it over to the wreck while Money Man, Katie, and a few others carry Roger to the Corvette. He picks up Roger's severed hand, drops it in the ice, then rushes back to his car with the bucket, setting it behind the driver's seat.

He glances at Katie, whose eyes are filled with tears. "I'll meet you at the hospital."

And with that, Mike gets into the car, slams the door, and speeds off, passing Schmitty as he arrives on his Harley.

"How bad is it?" Schmitty asks.

Katie doesn't answer. She just climbs onto the back of the motorcycle and clutches him tight like he's a life preserver.

In a panel van across from the real estate office, Detective Donald Neubeck huddles with half a dozen SWAT officers on benches, drinking lukewarm coffee out of paper cups and fighting boredom. There are several monitors hooked up, showing live video feeds from tiny cameras on the van and from other surveillance vehicles parked nearby.

Neubeck picks up a radio. "All units, check in."

A woman walking her dog down the street has a flesh-colored earbud that doubles as a microphone. She says, "Station two, all clear."

Two detectives are in a parked car on side street a block away. One of them grabs the mike. "Station three, clear."

Eric and Harry sit in another parked car, on another side street with a view of the real estate office. Eric takes the mike. "Station four, clear."

He puts the mike back in its cradle. Harry adjusts his junk, freeing a testicle pinched by his underwear. Eric looks away.

"Can't help it," Harry says. "I'm hung like a horse, with a ball sack the size of Santa's bag of toys. You try fitting that into bikini briefs and a pair of slacks."

"That's a picture I wish I could get out of my head."

"You're lucky I was able to talk the brass into letting a rookie like you come along on this with me."

"I appreciate it."

"You're going to learn a lot, starting with an introduction to the two most important tools of surveillance."

Harry opens the gym bag at his feet and takes out a thermos and plastic bag with a funnel on top, which he sets on the seat between them. He opens the thermos and pours himself a cup of coffee. Eric gestures to the device on the seat.

"What the hell is that?"

"A porta-potty. What goes in must come out. It's great to have at the movies, too. Never miss a scene that way."

Eric's cell phone rings. He checks the ID. It's Schmitty, which is odd, because the mechanic has never called him. It's always been the other way around. He takes the call with trepidation.

This can't be good news.

And it only takes three seconds for him to learn that it isn't.

✤ ✤ ✤

Eric rushes into the ER at Olive View–UCLA Medical Center to find Schmitty waiting for him in the corridor outside the waiting room. Schmitty reeks of pot.

"Thanks for the call," Eric says. "How is he?"

"He'll live. That's what matters."

"This is my fault. If I'd showed up for the race, he wouldn't be here."

"Jesus Christ. You and Katie were made for each other. Neither one of you can resist taking the blame for everything. Believe it or not, people are capable of doing stupid things entirely on their own."

"I'll keep that in mind."

"I hope so, because you're about to be tempted to do something really stupid right now."

Schmitty steps aside and gestures to the waiting room. Eric walks past him to see Katie and Mike standing together, their backs to him. He glances at Schmitty, who shrugs.

Eric marches into the waiting room. Katie turns and looks at him apprehensively. Without saying a word to Mike, Eric takes Katie by the arm and leads her aside.

"What is he doing here?" Eric asks.

She yanks her arm free from Eric's grasp. "Mike helped me when I needed him."

"Are you fucking him now, too?"

Without waiting for an answer, he launches himself at Mike, shoving him hard in the chest and slamming him back into the wall. Mike steps forward, ready to take a swing at Eric.

Katie rushes up, putting herself between the two men. "What are you two going to do? Start a fistfight right here? Grow up."

The two men back off just as the doctor approaches. He's in his late thirties and looks like he hasn't slept in two months. He directs his attention to Katie.

"Where are the boy's parents?"

"His mother is in New Zealand. I'm his cousin. I'm responsible for him now."

The doctor nods. He doesn't like it, but he's stuck with it. "You can see him, but only for a minute. We're about to take him into surgery."

Katie, Mike, Eric, and Schmitty follow the doctor back to the examination area, where Roger is lying on a bed. He's hooked to an IV and an EKG. He's pretty drugged up, his stump wrapped in bandages. He looks like a frightened child.

The three men stand at the back of the room.

Katie goes up to the bed, leans over Roger, and gently strokes his cheek.

"What were you thinking?"

"I figured it's building a car that's hard. Driving one is easy." His voice is scratchy and weak. "I guess I was wrong."

"You didn't have to do it."

"Someone had to, or the bank takes it all."

"It's just a garage," Katie says.

Roger glances at Mike, Eric, and Schmitty, then looks back at her. "It's our home."

The doctor comes in again, accompanied by two nurses and an orderly.

"We're ready for him in the OR. I'll find you in the waiting room when it's over," the doctor says. "Get comfortable. It's going to be a while."

Roger is wheeled away past them. Mike slips out at the same time. Eric turns to go, but Katie takes his hand.

"Please stay with me."

He's tempted, because he's not a heartless man, but then he remembers seeing the muscles on her naked back tensing up as she fucked the banker, how it felt to hear him moaning under her. And there's the stakeout he abandoned, the cops who are out there waiting to make an arrest, one that could change his career.

"I can't."

"Just for a little while."

"I have to go," he says abruptly, turning and leaving. She stares at his back until he goes. Schmitty steps up and puts his arm around her.

"I'm not going anywhere."

She hugs him, rests her head on his shoulder, and begins to cry.

"You will. The men in my life always leave me too soon."

Wolf is in Gargolov's sparkling clean, brightly lit garage, working alone under the hood of his yellow Mustang, tinkering with the engine, when Mike storms in, moving towards him like a laser-guided missile.

Wolf turns around and Mike decks him. It's a cheap shot. The bald thug takes the punch like it was a tickle and fires back with a hammer-fist into Mike's face that splits his lip and drives him back against a pillar.

Mike recovers fast, driving his fist deep into Wolf's gut and following up with a right hook that sends the thug stumbling back into the worktable.

Wolf grabs a tire iron and takes a swing at Mike with it. Mike ducks under the swing and sweeps Wolf off his feet with a swing kick. Wolf falls to his knees and drops the tire iron. Mike gets behind him, puts his knee to the small of Wolf's back, and begins to strangle him with the tire iron.

Mike hears the click of a gun being cocked behind his head.

"Let him go, please," Gregor Gargolov says calmly. He standing right behind Mike, close enough to whisper in his ear, so he can speak softly. Somehow, it's even more menacing that way.

But Mike doesn't ease up. "He took a kid's hand tonight."

"Then tonight the kid has become a man."

"A crippled man."

"Every man has scars, and your friend will learn from his that you never leave an opponent in a position to come after you again," Gregor says. "In Kiev, there are a lot of one-handed men who once knew me."

Mike releases Wolf, pushes him to the floor, and tosses the tire iron, turning around so that he's looking defiantly into Gregor's face down the barrel of the gun.

"That's good advice, Mr. Gargolov. Give me an ax and I'll teach this asshole the same lesson."

Gregor lowers his gun and shrugs. "I would, but he's my wife's nephew."

"Lucky you."

"Lucky him." Gregor grins and puts his arm around Mike like they are old pals. "I like you, Mike."

"I'm not real fond of you right now."

"Maybe this will change your mind." Gregor leads Mike to the Nissan GTR, gleaming under the halogens that light the garage. "The Japanese call this car Godzilla because it obliterates the competition. Now it's yours, ready to race."

"I don't think so."

"You don't like the car?"

Mike glares at Wolf, who is gasping for breath on the floor. "I don't like the people who work for you."

"Because they remind you of who you are. Working for men like me is the only way you will ever get what you want as quickly as you want it."

"My needs have changed."

"You have expensive tastes in cars, in women ... How long do you think it will be before your rich girlfriend gets tired of slumming with you?"

So Gregor's been watching him. That takes Mike aback, but only for an instant. He wipes the blood off his face with the back of his hand. "There are plenty of women who like it cheap and dirty."

"Thank God for that," Gregor says, removing his arm from Mike's shoulders and facing him. "So you're going back to delivering pizzas on that cute little scooter of yours."

"That's the plan."

Gregor laughs. "Who are you kidding, Mike? You won't get rich that way."

"I won't go to prison, either."

Gregor reaches into his pocket, takes out a wad of cash, and shoves it into Mike's shirt pocket. "This is an advance. Buy yourself some clothes that don't have a phone number on the back. Your father was one of the best wheelmen that ever was. You will be, too."

"You've done your research."

"I like to know who I am in business with. You'll race for me, and to pay for that privilege, you'll also drive some getaway jobs."

Mike angrily reaches for the money in his pocket, but before he can take it out, Gregor raises his gun and places the barrel against Mike's forehead.

"If you take that money out of your pocket, you will insult me deeply."

"That's the last thing I want to do."

"It certainly will be."

Mike stuffs the money back into his pocket and pats it. Gregor lowers his gun.

"Tomorrow you're going to take Marcus, Axel, and Clem to pick up some escrow documents for me," Gregor says. "You may need to bring them back in a hurry. I'm sure you'll do fine."

Gregor smiles, gives Mike a gentle slap on the cheek, and goes back to his office.

Mike glances at Wolf staggering to his feet, then licks the blood off his teeth and walks out.

Katie and Schmitty have spent the night sitting in the hospital waiting room in uncomfortable chairs. They are bleary-eyed from boredom and sleeplessness and queasy from eating a vending machine breakfast of candy bars, tortilla chips, and extruded coffee.

If this waiting and worrying go on much longer, they might have to check in as patients themselves.

The doctor finally comes out, looking like a zombie from *The Walking Dead* in sweat-stained scrubs.

It's not a sight that inspires confidence and hope.

Katie and Schmitty immediately stand up, their faces etched with concern.

"How did it go?" Katie asks, her voice scratchy.

"Roger came through the surgery very well and is in the recovery room," the doctor says.

"Does that mean he will be able to use his hand?"

"It will be months before we know how much sensation and mobility he'll regain. But don't count on him ever becoming a concert pianist."

Schmitty nods. "We appreciate what you've done, Doctor. Thank you."

"Go home and get some rest," the doctor says.

"Same to you, Doc," Schmitty says. "You look like hell."

"Feel like it, too." The doctor walks away.

Schmitty turns to Katie. "I'll tow the Ford back to the garage."

She nods, in a kind of daze. Now that Roger has come through, she has to face the painful reality that this new day brings. "I'm going to stay here until he wakes up. Then I'll come back to the garage. I have to pack up my things before the bank comes tomorrow morning."

Schmitty pats her on the back. "I've been around a long time. And here's what I've learned. Surviving is all that counts. You're a survivor."

She has no idea what that means, or why she should be encouraged by it, but she gives him a halfhearted smile and a nod, watches him go, and then slumps into one of the chairs, resigned to the inevitable.

Eric has also spent the night sitting. He's been in the unmarked police car all night with Harry, parked across the street from the real estate office. Harry has slept most of the time, but Eric had no trouble staying awake. He had way too much on his mind.

But now that Harry's up and a new team of detectives will be coming to relieve them soon, Eric is dozing. The sound of liquid streaming into a container wakes him up. He turns just as Harry zips up his fly and removes the porta-potty funnel from his crotch.

Harry offers the funnel and the huge bag of piss to Eric. "Want to take a morning whiz?"

"No, thank you."

"Good, because I think it's full up. I'm going to go empty this and get us some more coffee. Stay vigilant while I'm gone."

"Will do," Eric says.

Harry leaves. Eric stretches and looks in the rearview mirror, which is angled to see the real estate office that's behind him across the street.

Nothing is happening. About six employees arrived an hour ago, but no would-be home buyers or sellers have shown up. Real estate offices are not exactly hubs of excitement or activity.

The radio crackles.

"Heads up, everyone," Neubeck says. "We have a visitor."

An Audi A6 with tinted windows turns a corner onto the street and parks in front of the real estate office. Eric can't see any faces, but he can make out four figures in the car.

Mike is at the wheel. Marcus is beside him. Axel and Clem are in the backseat. The three thugs pick up long, wide gym bags at their feet.

"Keep the motor running," Marcus says. "This won't take long."

The three thugs get out of the car and march towards the real estate office, leaving Mike to sweat it out.

Neubeck is in a windowless panel van parked around the corner. He's watching the monitors and sees the three thugs enter the office. The SWAT members behind him are alert and ready to go. Neubeck picks up the mike.

"All units, maintain position. Nobody moves until they come out, unless shots are fired." Neubeck turns to the men in the van. "Lock and load."

The SWAT team put on their helmets, lower their visors, check their weapons, and prepare to deploy.

Mike glances into the real estate office and sees the three thugs pull AK-47s from their bags and herd the employees into the back room.

What the fuck?

❧ ❧ ❧

Eric buckles his seat belt and starts his car.

Harry Prendergast is walking down the street with his piss bag. He sees what's going down, takes cover behind a parked car, and pulls his gun.

The seconds are passing like hours. Mike nervously looks around. He sees a man on a bus bench, reading his newspaper and holding a finger to his ear, listening to something over an earpiece.

Shit.

Mike looks up the street and sees a parked car, the driver's back to him, smoke rising from the exhaust.

Shitty shit.

He glances in his rearview mirror and sees the nose of a windowless panel van parked at the curb. The van's engine is also running.

Shitty shit SHIT.

He puts the car into gear and floors it.

Marcus emerges from the back room to see the Audi speeding away, peeling rubber.

"Bastard!" he yells, brandishing his AK-47 and running towards the front door.

Neubeck sees his surveillance operation falling apart. He grabs the mike.

"We've been made! Move in! All units, *move in!*"

Eric floors it, screeching away from the curb. So does the other unmarked police car directly across from him. They brake to a stop, nose to nose, forming a wall of automotive steel blocking the street directly in front of the Audi, which is speeding towards them as if they aren't even there.

Mike turns from the impromptu roadblock at the last possible instant, his Audi fishtailing into a screeching half-turn that brings it sliding to a stop side by side with Eric's car, barely an inch apart from each other.

Eric and Mike turn their heads and look at each other.

Holy shit.

Now Mike knows that Eric, Katie's street racer, is a cop.

Now Eric knows that Mike, the pizza delivery guy, is a getaway driver for a mobster.

Now they are both fucked.

But Mike's shock quickly turns to amusement. Life just got a little more interesting—that's all.

He smiles at Eric. "See you around, buddy."

Mike backs up fast, remaining parallel to the two cop cars, and looks ahead at the next corner.

He sees a narrow sidewalk between a row of parked cars and a block of storefronts.

There's no way his car can fit on the sidewalk.

To his right, out of his passenger window, he can see Marcus coming out of the real estate office, aiming an AK-47 at him, and, farther down that same street, a ton of SWAT officers piling out of the panel van.

I'm a dead man anyway.

Mike floors the gas pedal, steering into the side of Eric's cop car, using the parked vehicle like a ramp.

The impact lifts the Audi up on the driver's side, its wheels rolling along the top of the cop cars.

✤ ✤ ✤

Eric ducks as his roof is flattened on the passenger side under the passing Audi.

Marcus opens fire, bullets riddling the Audi's hood, roof, and trunk as it drives over the police cars on two wheels.

Harry watches in amazement as the Audi rolls off the police cars and down the sidewalk balanced on only its two right wheels, edging sideways between the storefronts and a line of parked cars.

Unfuckingbelievable.

Mike is up in the air, the car rolling in its precarious angle down the sidewalk. The instant he reaches the next intersection, he turns the wheel to the left, and the car lands on all four wheels.

He's free. He lets out a banshee cry of victory and survival as he speeds away.

But in his wake, war is breaking out.

Eric is in his flattened car. He can hear gunfire. His door won't open, so he scrambles out his driver's side window and drops onto the street. He pulls his gun and looks up to see Marcus, Axel, and Clem out front, pinning the officers down under a spray of automatic weapon fire.

Harry stands up and saunters right out into the street with his porta-potty.

"Hey, assholes!" he yells and throws his piss bag into the air at them like a grenade.

❧   ❧   ❧

Marcus instinctively whirls around and shoots at the incoming object.

The porta-potty bursts apart, showering Marcus and his buddies with warm piss.

It's like God is taking a leak on them.

Harry uses the distraction to shoot Marcus in the head, which explodes like piñata full of whale blubber.

The shock and horror of being splattered with piss and brain matter is more than Axel and Clem can handle. They both drop their guns and surrender.

It's over.

It's also over for Katie's garage.

She pulls the tarp off the 1971 DeTomaso Pantera, the one her father rebuilt and her brother died in. She hasn't quite finished restoring it, and now it's possible she never will.

Schmitty walks up, holding an old toolbox. "I thought you were packing."

"I am. This and the tow truck are all that I'm taking."

"What about the Ford?"

She glances at the bashed-up Ford and the bloodstain on the crumpled hood. Nobody has bothered to wash it off.

"I'll sell it for parts, and sell whatever garage equipment I can, at the race tonight. At least we'll have some cash to take us wherever we're going."

"Then we're in good shape." He hefts his toolbox. "A tow truck and a toolbox is all a mechanic really needs."

❧   ❧   ❧

There's a party going on at the police station. Everybody is toasting Harry. His piss-bag showdown with three gunmen wielding AK-47s happened only a few hours ago, and it's already LAPD legend.

Harry could retire now a happy man.

Everybody is happy and in a celebratory mood except Eric, who slips away from the party unnoticed. Nothing has gone down the way he wanted it to. Not the arrest, not things with Katie. His dual lives, as a cop and a street racer, have both turned to shit, and he has no idea how to make either one of them right again.

Eric leaves the building and walks down the street, where he sees Mike Cassidy leaning casually against a black Nissan GTR that's parked in front of his Ford F-150 pickup.

Eric pulls out his gun and aims it at Mike, who doesn't even flinch. "You're under arrest."

"I don't think so," Mike says.

"I'm a police officer."

"Yeah, I know."

"I saw you participate in a robbery today, and trash two police cars, and I'm sure those aren't the only crimes you've committed."

"Probably not. But how are you going to explain how you recognized me?"

"From reading your arrest record."

"Uh-huh. And what were you doing looking at that?"

"I was researching Gregor Gargolov's known associates."

"You got onto Gregor because of Wolf, who you knew from all the illegal street racing that you've been doing."

"Prove it," Eric says.

"I'm not a cop. I don't have to prove anything. All I have to do is say it to your boss and the damage is done. Once you're outed as an illegal street racer, you are finished and your case falls apart."

"Are you threatening me?"

"That's a funny question coming from a guy pointing a gun at an unarmed man."

"You're a wanted felon. I'm taking you in."

"It can wait until after the race."

"What race?" Eric asks.

Mike slowly opens the driver's side door of his car and steps aside. "The one you're going to win tonight so Katie doesn't lose her garage tomorrow."

"Why don't you do it?"

"I've seen you drive. I can't win this race, but you can. I'll still be a crook tomorrow, but Katie won't have her garage anymore. If you love her, I don't know how you can stand by and let that happen."

Eric lowers his gun. "This isn't over between us."

"You've got that right."

Eric holsters his gun and gets in the car. Mike walks around the front of the car and gets in the passenger seat. Eric starts the car and revs the motor.

"Sweet," he says.

"It doesn't get any sweeter."

They've just found their common ground.

CHAPTER SIX

The Panorama Place mall, a big deal when it was built in 1961, was devastated by the 1994 Northridge earthquake and demolished one year later. But the tower's five-story concrete parking structure, which suffered only cosmetic damage, was left standing. The assumption was that a new, modern shopping center would be erected on the property and that the parking structure would be patched up.

But the mall was only 60 percent leased at the time of the quake, the two anchor department stores had been vacant for months, and that corner of Panorama City had already begun its steady decline into the hellhole that it is today, a place where nobody wants to live, much less shop. So nothing was rebuilt. It's amazing anyone even bothered to tear the wreckage down and haul it away.

The abandoned lot is now a weed-choked garbage dump, and the parking structure has become a magnet for skateboarders, drug addicts, graffiti artists, and car racing.

There must be a hundred people partying on the top floor amidst a dozen cars. Katie is here, too, working the crowd, showing people pictures of her garage equipment.

"All the equipment and tools have to go. Make me an offer. But it has to be tonight."

She's not getting any bites. She hears the growl of an unfamiliar car. Katie turns and sees a black Nissan GTR drift off the ramp that curls up from the fourth floor.

The GTR comes to a spinning, showy stop in front of Money Man. The windows are tinted almost as dark as the black paint job on the car. It's nearly impossible to see who is inside. To her astonishment, Mike gets out of the car and hands Money Man a stack of cash.

Wolf peels out of the crowd and gets right in Mike's face.

"You're racing me," Wolf says.

"Good. I hope you brought your ax."

"I'm going to cut off your balls with it when I win."

"If we're racing for balls, then you've got nothing to wager."

Wolf is about to lunge at Mike, but the Money Man steps between them.

"Save it for the race. First car to cross this line wins." He runs his foot along a red line painted on the ground. "The starting line is on the bottom floor. You take the winding ramp to the second level, drive across the floor to the next ramp, and take it to the third level, repeating the process until you get to the top. You got it? Or do I need to draw you both a picture?"

Neither man says a thing. Mike gets in his car and backs away. There's a flurry of bets as people practically climb all over themselves to get their wagers in to Money Man.

The GTR speeds down the curving ramp to the lower floor.

Katie watches Mike go, shaking her head with disgust. She can only imagine how much of his soul he had to sell to get that car, though she knows that she's in no position to judge. At least, unlike her, he wasn't stiffed on his transaction.

Mike peels away from the ramp on the second level and speeds across the open floor of empty parking spaces to one of the many graffiti-covered pillars. He comes to a screeching stop and gets out. Eric emerges from his hiding place behind the pillar and walks to the driver's side of the car, passing Mike on his way.

"Try not to scratch the paint," Mike says.

Eric gets behind the wheel, Mike slips into the passenger seat, and they head off to the opposite ramp and down to the bottom floor.

Money Man and half the crowd have regrouped on the ground floor of the parking structure.

Wolf's yellow Mustang and Mike's black GTR are side by side, separated by a pillar, engines rumbling. There's a long, open floor and a forest of concrete pillars between them and the narrow, winding ramp that curls up to the second level.

A woman with set of breast implants like NBA basketballs struts out to the starting line in a leather micromini and stiletto heels. Her bouncing breasts look like they're about to snap the flimsy, bulging halter top that's tied with taut spaghetti straps around her slender neck.

She steps in front of the cars, faces the headlights, and reaches behind her neck to untie the halter.

"Ready. Set." She drops her top. *"Go!"*

The cars roar past her, their wake lifting her halter off the floor, making it flutter like a busty butterfly.

The Mustang and the GTR speed across the open space towards the first, winding ramp.

Wolf hits it first, drifting up the curve, blocking any opportunity Eric has to speed past him.

Money Man and the others who are at street level crowd into the elevators and run up the stairwell to get to the top floor in time to meet the cars at the finish line.

The girl who started the race is in such a hurry, she forgets to pick up her halter top. When she runs, her breasts don't move at all.

Eric floors it on the open expanse of the second level towards the opposite ramp.

Wolf slams against the GTR, trying to force Eric into a pillar.

Eric yanks the wheel at the last second and the two cars fork on either side of the pillar, the GTR scraping it and setting off sparks. Mike winces.

"It's just a little ding," Eric says.

The Mustang is ahead again as they reach the ramp, but as they drift into the turn, the GTR edges past it.

Wolf bashes against him again, locking the two cars side by side in the tight space, both of them scraping the concrete edges of the ramp as they ascend.

Mike glowers at Eric, a shower of sparks outside the driver's side window illuminating his face.

"It's a brand-new paint job," Mike says.

"Stop whining. It's only a scratch."

The two cars burst out of the ramp on the third level at the same time. The floor in front of them is littered with the hulks of stripped, abandoned cars. It's an obstacle course.

The GTR and the Mustang break apart and weave around the junkers and the pillars.

Just as they are about to reach the next ramp, Wolf intentionally clips one of the junkers, sending it careening into Eric's path.

Eric steers around it, losing vital seconds.

Wolf surges ahead onto the next ramp, steering straight into the turn.

Eric floors it and wrenches the car into a drift, sliding sideways past Wolf in the tiny space between the Mustang and the wall, to take the lead.

It's a pretty slick move, and Eric is pretty damn proud of himself.

The instant the GTR slides sideways in front of the Mustang, Wolf surges forward and slams into the driver's side, T-boning the car and bulldozing it forward.

Now it doesn't seem like such a slick move after all. It seems like Eric drove right into a trap.

Mike looks over his shoulder, then back at Eric. "You want me to drive?"

"I've got everything under control."

Wolf pushes the GTR across the fourth floor like a battering ram.

"Yeah, I can see that," Mike says.

He can also see that Wolf is pushing their sideways car towards the low concrete wall ahead …

… and a four-story drop to the cracked asphalt below.

The son of a bitch wants to kill them.

Eric floors the gas pedal, but the tires can't get any traction against the sideways force.

They are going to hit the wall.

They are going to die.

"Hold on," Mike yells and hits the nitrous button.

The GTR blasts free, leaving nothing between Wolf, the low wall, and a long drop.

Wolf screams and slams on his brakes, but it's too late—he's got too much momentum.

The Mustang bursts through the concrete wall as if its made of plaster, and arcs into the air before tipping end over end and hitting the ground upside down, exploding in a fireball that can be seen for miles.

As the GTR arrives on the top floor, everyone is rushing to the far end of the structure to peer over the edge and see the flaming wreckage, which gives Eric the opportunity to slip out of the car unnoticed and make a run for the stairwell.

By the time everyone turns around, Mike is standing in front of his bashed-up car and Eric is gone.

The Money Man walks up to Mike with a thick wad of cash in his hand. "Is that how everyone drives in Tennessee?"

Mike gives him a cocky grin and takes his money. "With our eyes closed."

He spots Katie in the crowd, just long enough to register the relief on her face, before the sound of sirens approaching sparks a frenzy, everyone eager to get away before the cops and fire department arrive.

Mike is, too.

Nobody wants to be around to explain what happened to Wolf.

He gets into his dented, scratched-up car, makes a sharp U-turn, and charges back to the ramp.

On the top floor of another building, a penthouse apartment on Wilshire Boulevard, Nicole is relaxing naked in a bubble bath in a freestanding tub. The room is lit by candlelight, a bottle of champagne in an ice bucket on the floor beside her.

A man in a bathrobe comes in. He's in his fifties but wears the decades as well as Pierce Brosnan does, with the same elegance, wealth, and poise. He comes up to the tub and kisses her lips. She practically purrs.

"I've missed you, honey," she says.

"Me, too," Antoine smiles and sits on the edge of the tub. "Have you been good while I've been away?"

"Hell no." She smiles wickedly and pulls him into the water.

Katie is in her office, carefully taking down the family photos from the wall. She looks at each picture as she goes, savoring the memory for a moment, before packing it away in the box.

Mike comes in with a pizza box and places it on her desk. "I won this for you tonight."

"A pizza."

"There's extra pepperoni."

He opens the box. It's full of cash. She's stunned.

"That's a lot of pepperoni," she says. "What do you expect from me in return?"

"Tell the bank to go to hell, keep the garage open, and build more kick-ass street racers."

"Is that all?"

"Maybe let me drive them once in a while."

"We'll see," she says. But she keeps the money.

Mike turns and walks out. Katie smiles to herself and starts to put the photos back on the wall.

Mike drives the scratched-up, battle-scarred GTR into Gargolov's now dimly lit garage. When he gets out of the car, he sees Gregor standing in front of him, a gun held loosely at his side.

"You drove away and left my men behind, Mike. That wasn't very loyal."

"My only loyalty is to myself."

"Some might call that cowardice."

"I call it survival."

"You're pragmatic. I am, too. It's one of the things I like about you. But you're fortunate that Axel and Clem aren't talking to the police, or you'd be dead and they would be, too. That's how I survive." Gregor walks around the car, shaking his head at the damage. "You like banging up my cars."

"Wolf and I had a race. He lost more than his hand. Are you going to shoot me for that?"

"I thought about it, but accidents happen. That's life. Besides, I bet on you in the race. I won enough to give Wolf a nice casket and still have plenty of money left over."

"I'm glad, Mr. Gargolov, because it means we can part on good terms. I'm done working for you."

"You're an amazing driver, and thanks to you, I have no drivers left. Do you really think I'm going to just let you go?"

Gregor raises his gun and aims it at Mike, who shrugs.

"We're done either way."

Mike turns his back on Gregor and walks away. Gregor keeps his gun trained on Mike.

"Of all the places you could have gone after what happened in Tennessee, why pick California?"

"I wanted to work on my tan."

"It must run in the family," Gregor says. "Because your father fled here, too. I can find him for you."

Mike hesitates, just for a moment, then keeps on walking. "Great. Maybe he'll work for you."

Gregor smiles to himself and lowers his gun, letting Mike walk out unharmed.

"See you soon, my friend."

❖ ❖ ❖

It's a new day. The 1971 DeTomaso Pantera is in its place in the garage. Katie wistfully approaches her father's car and runs her hand along the hood. She gets inside, puts her key in the ignition, and starts the car.

She closes her eyes and listens to the engine. It sounds to her like her father's voice.

Someday you and I will go on a drive in this car together, Katie, nothing in front of us but the open road.

I can't wait, Daddy.

You don't have to. All you have to do is sit right here and close your eyes.

It's a fond memory. She smiles and opens her eyes to discover that she's not alone. Eric is standing beside the car.

"Going my way?" he asks.

"Probably. Get in and we'll see."

He gets into the passenger seat and closes the door. She looks at him tenderly.

"Thank you for what you did last night."

"I don't know what you're talking about," he says.

"Don't deny it. I know it was you who saved my garage. I was on the third floor during the race, behind one of the pillars. The way you drive is unique. It's like the way you—"

"Fuck," he says, interrupting her.

"I was going to say make love. There's a difference, you know."

"Really?"

He leans close and kisses her. That's when Mike comes in, wearing his Sal's Pizza jacket and carrying a pizza box.

"Can I get a lift?" he asks.

"No," Eric says.

"Sure," Katie says. "Hop on. But if you dent the car, I'll kill you."

Mike sits on the trunk. A moment later, Nicole comes into the garage. She's ravishing, as usual.

"Is there room for one more?" she asks.

Eric recognizes her immediately. It's the woman he ticketed. *Oh shit.*

She recognizes him, too, and smiles, amused at his misery.

"I don't usually pick up hitchhikers," Katie says with a smile, "but I'll make an exception in this case."

"Don't drive too fast," Nicole says, walking past Eric on her way to the back of the car. "You wouldn't want to get a ticket."

"Pushing it is what makes life fun," Eric says. "You ought to try it sometime."

Nicole sits on the trunk beside Mike. "Where are we going?"

"I don't know," Mike says. "But I'm glad you're coming along."

"Me, too, pizza man."

Eric looks at Katie, who smiles at him and then closes her eyes as she steers.

"Shouldn't you be watching where you're going?" he asks.

"I am."

They're on a narrow, seemingly endless stretch of empty highway across a wide-open plain, nothing in front of them but their dreams … and maybe a few deadly curves.

We'll see.

AUTHOR'S NOTE AND ACKNOWLEDMENTS

This a novelization of my screenplay for the 2007 film *Fast Track: No Limits,* which was shot in Berlin, starred Erin Cahill as Katie, Andrew Walker as Mike and Alexia Barlier as Nicolke, and doubled as the pilot for a proposed television series.

The movie was an international co-production that aired on television in Germany, France and Canada, and was released as a motion picture in many other countries around the world. For a while, things were looking good for the series. The production partners assembled a writers room, and the stories for the first season's episodes were plotted. But international coproductions are a complicated business, the deal fell apart, and the TV series didn't go forward.

Erin Cahill and Andrew Walker went on to great success, especially on the Hallmark Channel, where they have each starred in many movies. Alexia Barlier became a major TV star in France, where she's starred in several hit series, including *Falco, The Forest,* and *Sophie Cross.* And Pasquale Aleardi, who played Gregor Gargolov, most recently starred in the long-running German series *Kommissar Dupin.*

I am pleased to say that we have all stayed in touch over the last twenty years and have remained good friends.

I couldn't have written this novella, or have written and produced the motion picture that it is based upon, without the help of Sam Barer, who graciously shared his automotive knowledge, which I twisted to suit my creative needs, undoubtedly making scores of errors that make people who really know about cars cringe.

But neither version of this story—novella or movie—would have been possible without Hermann Joha, Heiko Schmidt, Axel Sand, Daniel Hetzer, Gavin Reardon, Victoria Burrows, Scot Boland, Christian Balz, Arianne Gambino, Elke Schubert, the entire *Fast Track: No Limits* cast and crew, the extraordinarily talented filmmakers and stunt people at Action Concept and, of course, my wife Valerie and my daughter Maddie.

If you'd like to see the movie *Fast Track: No Limits,* it's now available on Amazon Prime:

http://www.amazon.com/Fast-Track-No-Limits/dp/B004NM52SQ

or on DVD from Maverick Entertainment Group:

http://www.amazon.com/Fast-Track-Limits-Erin-Cahill/dp/B002HXVT8A

ABOUT THE AUTHOR

Photo © 2024 Linda Woods

Lee Goldberg is a two-time Edgar Award and two-time Shamus Award finalist and the #1 *New York Times* bestselling author of more than sixty novels, including the Eve Ronin series, the Ian Ludlow series, the Sharpe & Walker series, and seven books in the Fox & O'Hare series, which he coauthored with Janet Evanovich. He has also written and/or produced many TV shows, including *Diagnosis Murder, SeaQuest,* and *Monk,* co-created the Hallmark movie series *Mystery 101, and is a co-executive producer on the Acorn series Allie & Andi.* As an international television consultant, he has advised networks and studios in Canada, France, Germany, Spain, China, Sweden, and the Netherlands on the creation, writing, and production of episodic series. For more information, visit www.leegoldberg.com.

www.ingramcontent.com/pod-product-compliance
Lightning Source LLC
Chambersburg PA
CBHW050903180626
46814CB00007B/2873